A DAY WITH AN
EXTRATERRESTRIAL

A DAY WITH AN EXTRATERRESTRIAL

Lou Baldin

A Day with an Extraterrestrial

Published through Lulu Enterprises, Inc.

Copyright © 2008 Lou Baldin

First Edition.

ISBN: 978-1-4357-1961-3

Library of Congress Control Number: 2008904852

Truth is a double-edged sword, to get it we must give up something—like cherished illusions.

CONTENTS

Prologue   1

One Morning   3

Inside the Alien Ship   11

Outer Space   27

Super Structure in Deep Space   45

Shopping District   57

Space Gate Uranus   69

Memories from the Past   91

Human Town   113

One of the Moons around Uranus   127

Star Cluster   143

PROLOGUE

The narrative that follows is a bit fantastic and therefore some may choose not to believe such things possible. Nevertheless, I am compelled to tell this story and leave it to the readers how much, if any, of the story they wish to consider reality.

1

ONE MORNING

My name is Mike, my age early fifties. I am married, and have two children. My occupation is real estate, which I have been involved in for twenty-seven years. That morning I decided to take advantage of the beautiful weather and go to a park that was four blocks from my home. I had a quick breakfast at a restaurant before my leisurely walk prior to going to the office. Walking was a good way for me to keep in shape and gave me an opportunity to slow down and "smell the roses," as a wise old saying goes. Besides, I loved taking walks in the morning.

The park had the usual crowd of joggers, walkers, and a parent or two with children playing on the swings, nothing out of the ordinary. That was until approximately fifteen minutes into my stroll, when a man proceeded to pass me on the trail and I moved to one side to let him go by. Instead of passing me, the stranger slowed down to my pace and introduced himself as Milton.

Milton appeared to be an ordinary-looking Caucasian male, about forty-years-old with a full head of black hair and average build. He was a little taller than I was, approximately six-feet-tall and he was dressed in a jogging suit. Milton talked to me in a tone that seemed as if we were old friends from way back, but I did not know him.

"Hello Michael Vitorino Bolderini, remember me?"

"Hi … no, I don't. Who are you? How do you know my name?"

I could not believe that he used my full name. I never used my middle name. No one has used my middle name since I was a child back in Italy.

"I know a lot about you Michael. I have known you since your birth on this planet. I am not from Earth. I'm from another solar system located near the heart of this galaxy."

That sounded so absurd that I was not sure how to respond. I had talked about such phenomena as aliens and UFOs to others in the past myself. Now having heard it from this fellow, I could only imagine how foolish I must have sounded to friends and family members that I had mentioned my experience. Nevertheless, I immediately thought this person was a nut for talking as if he were a real extraterrestrial.

I have been aware of the UFO phenomena personally and experienced strange situations during my childhood and as an adult while in the military. Yet talking about it and hearing Milton speak openly about being from another planet brought the irrationality to the forefront for me and made me uncomfortable.

I opted to gloss over the irony of my awkward situation and attempted to bring the conversation with Milton politely to an end, or so I had hoped.

"Good to have met you Milton and we must talk again sometime about life in the galaxy, but I need to finish my walk and get back to my office. Have a nice day, Milton."

Having said that to him, I went from walking on the trail to a fast trot, fully expecting to leave Milton behind me as I sprinted away from him. After five or six minutes of running, I became winded and figured that I could safely resume walking again, foolishly believing that I had put enough distance between Milton and myself. To my horror, Milton had remained a few steps behind me the whole time—on my very heels! I had not noticed him until I slowed down, looked behind me, and nearly had a heart attack! He grinned at my startled look and said, "That's the Vitorino I remember, always trying to get away from me."

I shouted back with a slightly elevated voice, "What the hell does that mean? 'Always trying to get away from whom?' Who are you? And why are you following me?"

Usually I'm a calm and reserved individual and slow to anger, but something about that fellow elevated my blood pressure.

The stranger named Milton did not answer my query and did not stop following me. Therefore, I stopped dead in my tracks and demanded to know more about him and his motives for interrupting my walk that morning. However, he walked right past me and left me there seething on the verge of an outburst. I stood there a few seconds attempting to regain my composure and trying to make sense of why that person's actions irritated me so much. Yet, I could not understand why he ignored my simple questions when he was the one who started the strange conversation in the first place.

The tables had turned and he sprinted away from me. Suddenly, I was the one doing the following and chasing. I did my best to keep up with him because I was determined to get some answers, but I was not sure of my questions anymore. Milton seemed to delight in my puzzlement as he glanced back at me, sped up his pace, and jogged further away from me, as if he knew I would pursue him. And I did.

I was confused but irritation propelled me to seek out why he refused to give me a simple answer to my question. My loss of control made me feel awkward and silly. But not enough to keep me from pursuing and confronting a person that possibly was unstable. Here I was, a grown man, chasing another grown man over a name. Perhaps he was psychic, or he was an old acquaintance that I had forgotten about, but reason was not with me that morning. It was as if I had lost control of my will and was operating under some external power that had taken me over.

Milton continued to ignore me and as I gained on him, he sped off like a gazelle with surprisingly unlimited amounts of energy. My attempt to catch up to Milton was futile. I was too slow and feeling every bit of my half-century-old body. However, Milton made sure he did not lose me and slowed down whenever I slowed down.

The jogging trail stretched around the park and part of it went through a forested area that was out of view from the rest of the park.

That was where we were heading. After entering the trees and the cover they provided, Milton ran off the trail and disappeared into thick brush. About fifty feet into the forested area, I suspected perhaps an ambush from the possibly crazy Milton and stopped chasing him.

Having regained my senses, I decided to forget the whole thing and go back to the parking lot where my car was, and drive home. As I turned to leave, I noticed something shimmering brightly in the direction that Milton had run off. About two hundred feet from where I was standing, there was a blindingly bright object in the woods.

There was something next to the object, but it was difficult to see details in the object's glare. My curiosity propelled me to look with more determination to make it out. That is when I saw Milton. He was standing next to what appeared to be a flying saucer. The craft looked like a large metallic Frisbee with a slight bulge at the top, but flat on the bottom. It had no visible windows or doors that I could see from where I was standing. As my focus improved, the object began pulsating with assorted colors. Suddenly, it was as if something clicked in my head and I was able to see it more clearly. The ship had a familiar look and I was captivated by it, but I was not sure why. The ship hovered about three feet above the ground in a small clearing. Sunlight steamed through the trees and reflected off the metal creating an angelic glow.

My focus turned towards Milton and away from the craft. He was waving at me, gesturing for me to come over to him. I wanted badly to avoid his eyes, but he continued waving for me to approach him. There was no clear path to where he and the strange vehicle were located, in the thick brush and trees covering the whole area off the trail. I had no desire or intention of going anywhere near the space alien and his machine, regardless of the alluring qualities of his ship.

Believing I was in control of my movement, I attempted to turn back and walk in the other direction away from that hidden part of the park. Mysteriously, I somehow knew deep inside I could not walk away. I tried not to panic, thinking that perhaps if I remained calm I could fight the urge that was bombarding my mind to go toward the ship.

Remaining calm did not work and I suddenly realized that I could not move my feet. I could not go forward or backward. I was glued to the spot where I stood. Then a feeling of dread and despair came over me like a tsunami. I could not move my body, but I could move my head. I looked around and scanned the trail for other people on what was normally a busy walking trail. But there was no one and I was alone with Milton. The invisible force that held me began pulling me toward the ship as if I were riding an invisible conveyer belt. Then I heard a voice in my head that sounded like Milton's voice.

"Do not resist, Michael. This nightmare will soon pass."

Milton was speaking telepathically to me. I responded the only way I knew how.

"GOD HELP ME! Christ, what is happening to me?"

I yelled, but I could not hear any sound. The lack of sound coming from my lung-powered voice box was a very strange sensation and I did not like it. I was completely helpless as my body moved inexplicably in the direction of the ship.

The trail teaming with people earlier was now oddly empty. Apparently, that fellow Milton was somehow mentally manipulating the other people away from that section of the park. If true, that was astounding. Yet there was no other explanation for my being alone there.

I struggled with my emotions and just before my body reached the disk, I lost consciousness, but not completely. I was able to see myself as if I were out of my body and all around me was indiscernible and yet still clear to me somehow.

2

INSIDE THE ALIEN SHIP

A bluish vapor illuminated the inside of the craft like that of a fluorescent tube filled with electrified gas. A corridor wrapped around the interior perimeter where portholes (windows) gave a clear view of the outside and other parts of the park in exquisite detail. A wall on the opposite side of the windows concealed the mysterious interior of the alien craft. The windows were not apparent from the outside of the ship, but stood out as ovals from the inside.

The windows seemed to amplify the details of everything outside beyond the portholes. Items of interest for a person inside of the ship were prominently displayed on the window screen as if the window zoomed-in on exterior objects. The windows or the ship knows what a person looking through the window is focusing on. As I passed through the ship on the invisible conveyer belt that was pulling me or carrying me into the ship, I was not sure how I knew some of the details about the ship that suddenly appeared in my mind, as if old memories were awakened.

There were no noticeable doors into the craft or into the interior of the ship from the corridor. No seams or other hints to where doors might be located were apparent. There were only smooth rounded surfaces indicative of a highly advanced and flawless technology.

The disc interior was silent. Sound from the outside did not penetrate the ship and no sound from whatever powered the craft was noticeable. No sounds were apparent from other occupants; if there was anyone else inside besides Milton and me, they remained silent. I passed into the interior of the ship in a semiconscious state and telepathic briefings about the craft emerged in my mind—perhaps from Milton or a mechanism in the ship itself. Then I traveled into one of the spooky interior rooms.

QUARANTINE ROOM

I found myself standing upright, but I was not touching the floor, ceiling, or walls. I remained partially conscious and paralyzed in midair. My arms were at my sides as if I were standing at attention. The temperature in the room was cooler than the temperature in other parts of the ship and vapor came out of my mouth as if I were in a walk-in freezer at a butcher shop.

I could not see Milton. It appeared that I was alone, in the room. There were no visible instrumentation or control panels and no means of entering or exiting. The room was like a large cocoon. The compartment was a bluish-white and reminded me of an electrified cloud. Moments after I entered the room guided by the invisible force that had plucked me from the park, a small, spherical object about the size of a golf ball and glowing with intense colorful light emerged from one of the walls. It permeated through the wall without leaving an exit hole. It buzzed around my head like a large mosquito and spiraled down and around me like a corkscrew to my feet and back up again. It moved at amazing speed, scanning my whole body and neutralizing bacteria on my skin and clothing. That bit of info came from an earlier memory from previous encounters that seeped into my consciousness. During the whole procedure, I remained semi-conscious and fully dressed in the clothing I wore that morning.

The ball then moved to my head and touched the very top of my skull, spinning me like a washing machine on spin cycle. The spinning lasted several seconds and then I became stationary. My body moved to a horizontal position while I remained stiff as a board, arms at my side and floating about two feet above the floor of the room.

The mysterious ball departed the room in the same manner that it entered, but exited through the floor, as if an apparition. Then Milton's voice came into my head.

"Wake up, Michael."

Milton telepathically communicated with me from an unknown location in the ship.

Upon hearing Milton's command, I instantly opened my eyes and regained full consciousness. Yet, I felt I was more conscious of my surroundings when I was in my semi-conscious state, where details seemed much clearer. Groggy and dizzy I responded to Milton verbally with a question.

"Where am I Milton?"

"You are in my ship."

"Why am I in your ship and why can't I move?"

"You will regain full equilibrium shortly, after your brain makes the necessary adjustments that were uploaded into it. That will allow you to move about the ship in what you would consider a 'normal' manner. You will be able to orient yourself to up, down, and sideways, even though no such thing exists in space or in this ship, even while it remains parked inside the Earth's atmosphere."

At that moment, my body floated down and touched the floor of the ship. I jumped to my feet with incredible ease as if I were an accomplished acrobat.

"Are we in space, Milton? I feel no gravity pulling on my body and I have so much energy. I think I could run a marathon without getting winded, like I did earlier in the park."

Most of my fear was gone and I felt great and filled with vigor. I spoke to Milton vocally as if he were standing in the room with me. Yet, I was alone in the room.

"The ship hasn't moved and remains in the park at the very spot where I picked you up, Michael."

"How long have I been in the ship? My watch is not working for some reason and I assume it stopped when I entered the ship, perhaps due to magnetic interference or whatever makes your ship operate. Anyway, it stopped at 8:15 AM; what time is it now, Milton?

"It's exactly 8:17 AM, Michael."

"NO WAY! I feel as if hours have passed. You must be incorrect, Milton. Did your watch stop, too?"

"I never make mistakes and I don't need a watch. It's not even possible that I'm wrong. Only two minutes have passed since I brought you into the ship and prepped you for a little trip."

"I don't want to go on any trip with you. Please let me out of here! You have no right to take me anywhere without my consent and you are breaking the law by holding me here. Where is the exit to this ship, Milton?"

"There are no exits or doors on my ship unless I create them for you. You may only enter and leave a room or the ship if and when I allow it. Besides, I'm not under any human jurisdiction and your laws don't apply to me."

"Fine, can you please create a door for me so that I can leave this ship and get back to my normal life that you so rudely interrupted? Will you please allow me to leave this ship, Milton? I promise I will not press charges if you let me go."

I did not wait for Milton to respond and ran toward one of the walls of the room in which I was caged and body-slammed against it. I bounced back off the wall in slow motion as if I had hit a marshmallow and gently fell back to the soft floor. I got up and tried again several times, but finally gave up, though not from exhaustion. I had plenty of energy, but it was as if I were inside a padded cell. I realized the absurdity of my situation and nearly broke out in laughter as if I had gone mad!

"This is insane!" I yelled at the top of my voice. I kept looking for a hidden door. What baffled me the most was how did I get in the ship in the first place and then into that room? I was trying to figure out how Milton got me in there when he was not even in there with me, yet he talked to me as if he were.

"I put you in there and you can only leave when I tell you that you can leave. Do not get excited, Michael. You are not my prisoner for long and I intend to let you out of that room, but not out of the ship just yet. Now, walk forward and place your hand on the wall in front of you, the one you have bounced off several times, and then imagine yourself walking through the wall."

"You are crazy, Milton. The walls are like solid rubber or something. Why don't you just push a button, or whatever it is you do, and create an opening for me and stop with the mind games?"

"We don't use buttons or switches or magic wands, although some of our stuff works like magic. At least in your mind it looks like magic because it is not part of your human reality. As for mind games, well, life is a mind game. Now, do what I said and walk through the wall."

I placed my hand on the very spot I bounced off several times. Rolled my eyes as if "what's the use," but that time my hand passed through the wall as if there were nothing there. I walked through the wall bewildered by it all. I took a closer look at the wall opening, that formidable barrier that kept me prisoner, and found it was paper thin and ethereal in consistency. There was nothing there but the illusion of a wall!

CORRIDOR

I saw a row of windows circling around the craft exactly the way I remembered seeing them when I first entered the ship that morning. I went up to one of the windows and looked out. I could see the trees and a small section of the trail from where I had been taken. There were people walking on the trail, but no one was aware of the alien ship sitting off in the woods only a few feet from them. The people went about their lives oblivious to the supernatural situation in which I found myself entangled. I was envious of their freedom, as they moved along the trail and the park lost in their own little worlds of human delusions.

Not a single person noticed that I simply vanished while walking on the trail alongside them. Not that I would have noticed if it were someone else that went missing. Most of us come to the park alone and leave the park alone, as we do in life when we are born and when we die. I became somewhat philosophical during my apparent life review given to me while caged inside the alien ship that morning, and it made me uncomfortable. I was in no mood for existential reflection. I wanted out of that crazy ship or nightmare that I was stuck in!

It boggled my mind that no one could see the ship when I could see each of them perfectly and clearly through the ship windows.

"Why can't anyone see the ship, Milton? I saw it."

"I let you see the ship. It remains invisible to all unless I unlock it in their mind, as I did for you."

"Lucky me!" I shot back sarcastically. I pushed on the wall space between the windows thinking that perhaps I might find a wispy barrier to fall through, with no luck. I pried on one of the porthole windows with my car keys, but nothing happened, not even a scratch or rip. The material seemed indestructible. I pounded on the glass with clasped fists and even banged my head against the glass, but it did not hurt the glass or my head.

The portholes were spaced about a foot apart and I went from one to the next, testing all of them by hitting them with extreme frustration. Then suddenly, one of them moved. I thought that perhaps I had found a flaw in that porthole. I scrutinized it looking for hinges or seals that might have come loose and concentrated all my energy on that one window. I pushed it and smacked it with fists, feet, and my head repeatedly and finally success! Or so I thought.

During my one-man rampage against that porthole, it suddenly shot away like a large Tidally Wink and landed on another spot of the ship's exterior wall. That was not what I had expected to happen and I was left standing there dumbfounded. I was in a freaking cartoon world! The hole from where the porthole lifted away filled in instantly as if the skin of the ship were made of a liquid-crystal type material, the kind that is used in advanced electronic timepieces and television screens. However, the human version of liquid crystal has no strength whatsoever, unlike the stuff in that ship. Where the porthole landed, the liquid crystal (for lack of a better word) was displaced and a new view to the outside appeared through it. Then all the portholes went into a shuffle mode and rearranged themselves back to their proper order. It was bizarre!

"This ship is peculiar to the max, Milton! So fantastically peculiar, it almost makes me giddy except for the fear factor, which spoils the fun. I can walk through paper-thin walls that are stronger than steel and soft as marshmallows and the windows can move to any location without leaving a hole. How is that even possible?

"My ship uses a highly advanced technology; this technology is in use on many other planets, which are only a few notches above what you have here on Earth. What seems magical and bizarre to you is common everyday stuff in the countless civilizations inhabiting this galaxy. You are not dreaming, nor are you in a nightmare. You are in fact in a place that is much more real than anything you will ever experience in your human existence on Earth."

"I don't even know how to respond to that, Milton. You are talking stuff way over my head. So, are you 'people' like us humans here on Earth, only more advanced than we are, Milton?"

"We are not quite people like you humans are, not in the sense of so-called intelligent life on planets like Earth. There are many shades and levels of existence and some shades or versions are like 'people' here on Earth. But I don't fall into those categories."

"Why can't I see you, Milton? Are you invisible? Was your 'form', your 'appearance', on the walking trail not the real you? You looked and talked like a so-called 'intelligent' human when you approached me during my walk this morning, Milton."

"You can see me if I choose to show myself, but what you will see when you do see me is only window dressing and not the real way I look, whether it be in a 'human' uniform or an 'alien' uniform. But you cannot see me as I really am, at least not yet. I'm not your average Joe and nothing at all like what you saw on the trail this morning."

Milton communicated telepathically and received my words directly from my mind, even though I talked through my vocal cords and mouth. Because thoughts are faster to pick up than the sound coming from my vocal cords, Milton knew my thoughts before I could vocalize them! That was a huge disadvantage for me during conversations with him.

Without warning, Milton popped into the corridor out of thin air a few feet in front of me. At first, he appeared to be an apparition which quickly solidified, or fazed into my reality, not that I knew what reality was anymore. He was not the human-looking Milton I chased back in the park. He was altogether a far different and spooky-looking creature from space, and beyond description. I did manage to remember certain features about him before my brain froze up, stalled, and then plunged me into a state of physical and mental shock once the sight of his insidious-looking carcass fully registered in my mind.

He was short, about three feet tall, maybe less. He had a bulbous head that was not proportional to his body, but much larger, as if he had a tumor swelled up inside his cranium. His arms were thin, as were his legs. His body was trim, yet a bit pudgy in the mid-section. I did not notice how many fingers or toes he had, or if he had a skintight suit. He did not seem naked or dressed. He simply looked incredibly different from what we humans are accustomed to seeing. Ears did not protrude from his head, only small holes where ears would be. Dominating his figure were large, dark, penetrating eyes, which looked as if they could paralyze a charging herd of wild elephants with one glance. The rest of his facial features were hardly noticeable due to his eyes, which did not allow me to focus on other features very well. Nevertheless, I managed to remember some details. He had a tiny mouth that was too small for talking. The nose was two narrow slits. His skin color was a shade of dark blue with white iridescent splotches that moved as if in a liquid below a translucent layer of skin. The skin was smooth like glass with no wrinkles or scales and he had a glow around him like an electrified aura or shield that emanated from his body.

I blurted out a few words to Milton before the full affect of his appearance knocked the wind out of me.

"Milton, I presume? Man, you look totally unnatural and freaky and nothing like I ever expected!"

The hair on the back of my neck stood straight out like the stiff bristles of a porcupine. Adrenalin surged through my body and overwhelmed my nervous system. I remained conscious but my mind became a jumbled haze of mental images and thoughts.

As my mind turned into mush like carrots in a blender, I did not fall to the floor. Instead, my body went limp and I hung suspended in midair like a puppet on strings. Milton then touched my head at the temple area with his strange looking, dangly finger. Or perhaps he was holding some alien object he might have been clutching and I regained a semblance of consciousness on some other level than normal.

I attempted to convey my feelings to Milton and managed to stutter a few intelligible words.

"Milton—you scared—the crap—out of me—and you still do—what have you done to my mind? Everything is a jumbled up blur of madness."

"Michael, you are not ready to see me in any other form than human form. We program human brains that way, for reasons I will get into later. However, I will alter that program in your mind today so that you can communicate with me without losing control of your consciousness. Nevertheless, I will remain in the background and out of sight most of the time, so as not to interfere with what we are going to do with you during this encounter."

Milton vanished from before me and I instantly regained my faculties and composure. I was completely relaxed, more so than when he first entered the room and overwhelmed me with his appearance.

"Why don't you appear to me in human form and eliminate the potential for the shock factor and mental holocaust? Wouldn't that make things easier for all concerned, especially me?"

"Human bodies, and we use a modified version of the human body such as the one you saw me in on the walking trail this morning, are not equipped to perform well on this ship. The body I appeared in that totally freaked you out incorporates advanced designs and has multiple uses, including the shock affect that you received from it. It is an extremely versatile machine built for the environment inside our types of vehicles. Those bodies are suited well for our work in this solar system, specifically when dealing with humans and other physical and non-physical forms of entities. We usually block the memory from those we interact with so that our looks are not generally an issue or a concern to our guests."

"That's all well and good for you and those who get their memories blocked, but from my perspective your appearance makes for a great horror costume. That is very distracting for those like me who remain conscious of the ordeal. Are you going to block my memory of how you look once I leave your ship so that I don't have nightmares?"

"I will block some of your memory of me and certain other things you will see and experience today, so that your normal life is not completely disrupted or impaired. However, you will get to retain various memories depending on how you react to each situation we put you through. I am not in a body now. I am like a spirit. The body that you saw me in, which gave you mental indigestion, is like a space suit for us. Have you noticed how creepy NASA spacesuits look? Can you imagine how someone unfamiliar with them and at a lower technological stage might react to seeing one? Granted, we are much scarier, but same principle."

"How are you able to see me, Milton? Are there cameras throughout your ship? Or are you in the corridor with me now and using some kind of cloaking device?"

"I'm not in the corridor with you. I have a special place in the ship where I remain while in spirit form. There are no cameras looking down on you or in any other place inside this craft. But I am fully aware of everything inside the ship, as well as things outside of the ship. I have more than the five senses you humans have."

"Are you a god, Milton?"

"No."

"How much time has passed since you disrupted my life and brought me to this point of mind obliteration?"

"That time thing is not important for now, but less than thirty minutes have passed since the start of the adventure you are now in. Does that ease your 'obliterated mind' some?"

"Perhaps an adventure for you, Milton, but not for me. Can you speed up time and do whatever it is you have to do so that I can get out of here and on with my real life back in the real world? I do have a life you know!"

"I'm taking us up into Earth's stratosphere. Are you up for that? Ha ha, get it? 'Up for that.' Never mind. Humans never get my humor, perhaps because I obliterate their minds. Anyway, if you wish to watch our ascent into space, go to one of the portholes and take a peek out the window and be prepared to be utterly amazed and jolted out of your sheltered human bubble of a life."

The instant I began to walk towards one of the portholes as Milton directed, the ship shot straight up at a phenomenal speed. Yet, I felt absolutely no motion, nor did I lose my balance while I was walking from window to window. I looked out one of the windows just in time to see the treetops and the park turn into insignificant specks. I watched the continents shrink and the oceans enlarge and my mind expanded tenfold. Then the ship stopped dead cold somewhere above Earth without me splattering up against the ceiling of the ship. In a matter of seconds, we had traveled from the park and into space without any vibrations or turbulence, as I had experienced inside of airplanes and on space rides with my children at Disney World. We stopped abruptly without any semblance of gravitational G-forces on my body whatsoever. That was certainly not the physics I had learned about while at school in the real world. I was flabbergasted at what I saw outside the porthole windows!

I did remember past encounters with otherworldly entities, but most of it was blocked or hidden between normal human memories. Those mysterious memories became much clearer that day while in Milton's ship.

In the old days people were accustomed to the gods interfering in their lives; the gods were real back then.

3

OUTER SPACE

I gazed upon a huge, blue planet with its wisps of white clouds running across it and a full moon off in the distance not quite behind the Earth. I nearly wet my pants from the excitement of that sight. The awesomeness was numbing and incomprehensible for my little human brain. This had to be real. It felt and looked more real than my so-called real life back on Earth—but how could that be possible? I wondered.

I never tear up easily, but I became outright emotional and choked up with joy from what I was seeing. I walked around the ship stopping briefly to catch a glimpse out of the other portholes, each harboring a unique and spectacular view of the heavens. I saw the moon in a new light and from a new perspective. "Magnificent" became my mantra and I repeated it in my mind as I gazed out the windows in pure awe. I looked into the darkness of space—not so dark up there. It was lit up like a Christmas tree, with billions of glittering stars in our glorious and majestic Milky Way galaxy, which sported endless numbers of stars, some gathered in globs of dust and the hot matter of the universe. Space is an endless sea of magical luminosity.

Other planets in our solar system were prominent in their orbits around the sun, their vague profiles magnified by the mysterious glass in the portholes. I also discovered that I could look directly at the sun without it affecting my eyes. However, that experience bordered on disturbing because we humans learn early not to stare into the blinding sun. That was not a danger from inside that ship. The clarity and the details exceeded anything from Earth-based telescopes and other instruments that astronomers used for peering into the glowing soul of our nearest star.

I could not comprehend what I felt when I looked into the sun that morning, but it had a profound effect on me and I still do not comprehend fully what that effect was. The glass in the portholes amplified objects such as stars and planets and at the same time screened out harmful radiation from the sun. I was completely mesmerized looking directly into the sun. It was addictive and nearly orgasmic, yet my mind continued to remind me to turn away from peering into the face of pure electrifying energy. Nevertheless, I simply could not get enough of the view to satisfy my desire for more. Milton told me to indulge-away, but "don't try it at home."

"Have you seen enough, Michael? Should I return you to the park now so that you can get on with your boring life?"

"No! I do not want to return yet. Please...Let me see more—I want more!"

"Then you shall have more, but first you will need to explore some things that are locked away in your head. I will help you find what you need to know in order to continue with this journey."

While Milton talked, I remained fixated on the marvels of space and moved from one portal to the next as if this were my only chance to suck it all in. Then an opening in the wall behind me drew my attention away from the windows.

"Walk through the opening, Michael."

I reluctantly tore myself away from the portholes and entered the opening and the opening closed behind me.

MEDIA ROOM

I gazed down an immense hallway stretching to infinity and with doors on both sides of the passageway. I was speechless. The ship was small; it looked about 30—40 feet in diameter from the outside at most. At least that was my impression of it when I first saw it at the park that morning. So how could it be so large inside? The first thing that came to my mind was that the small ship must have docked with a larger, invisible mother ship, or perhaps an alien space station that was in Earth's orbit. However, I did not see any space station from the portholes. My second inclination was that Milton's ship was a holographic rat maze and I was the rat.

"We are not docked to a larger ship or a space station, Michael, nor have you entered into another ship. You remain in the same ship that you entered at the park this morning. And Michael, you are not a rat in a maze—or are you?"

"I don't know what I am, but I'm feeling very small and more confused than I ever have in my entire life. There are dozens of doors in this hallway. What is that about? You said there were no doors on this ship, Milton."

"Maybe I did say that, but I am allowed to change my ship and the rules if I feel the need and I feel the need. However, feel free to explore and ask as many questions as you wish and I might even answer a few of your questions."

"Please tell me that more than an hour has passed since we left the park, Milton."

"That's the best you have? You sure are concerned with time, Michael. Relax! Time may be relevant in your world, Michael, but not in mine, and right now you are in my world."

"Perhaps time is not important to entities such as you, Milton. You are in possession of a magical spaceship and share power with the gods, but for those of us stuck on Earth with little means of understanding beyond our petty survival instincts, time is very important. But concerning time and on a lighter note, will it speed up now that I'm having fun?"

"Time is an illusion and has little significance in this realm you are in now. In space, there is no such thing as minutes and hours, which are simply divisions of one Earth day, which is a division of one Earth year. The twenty-four-hour day has no importance whatsoever outside of Earth's surface."

I walked down the hallway glancing at the doors. They looked the same as the doors that we have in our houses and buildings back on Earth: Rectangular slabs with hinges and doorknobs, nothing special to write home about, except they were on an alien spaceship. They looked out of place on Milton's "Magical Mystery Tour" of a spacecraft, and made me wonder if the Beatles knew more about alien spaceships than they let on. The inner hallway was even more confusing because it looked like it belonged inside an old mansion with east and west wings, adorned with the occasional columns and statuary. I had a creepy feeling about the statuary. Perhaps they were alien creatures or android-type entities standing as guardians awaiting orders from Milton. The walls, floor, ceiling, and doors in that hall were bright white and metallic looking, but did not have the feel of metal when I touched the walls. The material was soft like skin or expensive leather. That hall, as well as the outer hall with the windows, was not dark and mysterious. It was well lit and mysterious.

"Which one of these doors is the bathroom, Milton?"

"No bathroom on this ship, Michael. If you should have a problem with your plumbing, there is a cleanup room you will be taken to by scary-looking androids. Those plumbing problems usually only happen when people are first abducted and they loose control of their modesty—from the sheer hair splitting fear that comes over them. Do you remember when you were a boy, Michael? And you picked up a turtle and the turtle peed because it thought you were going to eat it? Same difference."

"Turtles aside, I have never heard of a place that didn't have a bathroom. What do you do, Milton, when you have to go?"

"I never need to go. The body I use when I use it is designed differently than human bodies. We do not consume food or drink as you do, unless we are in a human copy and hanging out on Earth with humans. Then we only eat and drink in order to blend in with those around us. We do not like sticking out, if you know what I mean. We then choose to use the facilities so as not to give ourselves away. We can metabolize the food and drink completely away; no waste, no mess, no trace."

"I guess that means there are no snack machines?

"Are you hungry and thirsty, Michael? Or just whining and complaining?"

"No I'm not hungry. Yes, I am whining, but what happens when I get hungry and or need a drink of water? It would be nice to know if those things are available and where they might be found."

"When you get hungry, we will stop at a fast food restaurant. I hear Earth has plenty of them. However, you will not need to eat or drink during your stay in the ship. Your body uses the minimum of energy, less than when you are sleeping. You already had your potty break when I appeared to you in my space alien uniform. You were like that turtle I described."

"I don't remember doing anything like that and my clothes are dry and clean."

"We have dry-cleaners on this ship. They are open twenty-four-seven and they are extremely efficient, don't you agree?"

I did not answer I tried to clear my mind of the whole thing and focused on choosing a door to enter. After milling around, uncertain of why I was trying to decide on a door when all of them looked the same, I made my selection and walked through one of them. The room I entered glowed brighter than the hallway and it was like walking into a huge spotlight. At the center of the room was a single theater seat and on the wall opposite the door I entered was what appeared to be a movie screen. The room was not visually large looking, yet it felt huge a sensation that is difficult to describe. Many of the small spaces inside the ship did not feel small or cramped.

The theater seat was the first sitting apparatus I had encountered thus far. In zero gravity, sitting really did not make sense anyway. This particular ship had zero gravity even when it was on Earth, so why bother with seats. I was never fatigued while in the ship; instead, I had more energy than ever and had no desire to sit.

Lack of gravity was not an obstacle either. I was able to walk as if I were on Earth without the assistance of gravity shoes. I did feel light as a feather, but also did not float around precariously as do astronauts in the International Space Station.

I wondered if all this were an elaborate scheme to make me believe I was in space. Certainly, with our current technology a covert operation could have rigged the portholes with sophisticated computer generated graphics, which projected onto the screens made to look like windows on a flying saucer. Then again, why would a secret government agency go to the expense and trouble to make little old me think I was in contact with extraterrestrials?

I stepped toward the seat in that room, but before I could sit down, a strange creature entered the room. It was carrying what looked like a spacesuit and a space helmet in its arms. The creature might have been one of the statues that I passed in the hallway. It was about the same size, but Milton never commented when I asked him about it.

"Put on the spacesuit, Michael, you are about to go for a walk in space."

"I'm not sure I am ready for a space walk, Milton! Don't I need some basic instructions first? Spacewalking seems dangerous. How will I know if I put the spacesuit on correctly? I did not mean to doubt that I was in space, Milton. I keep forgetting that you can scan my mind and pick up on my doubts and fears—shit!"

"Your little helper will make sure the spacesuit is on right. I think it will be safe to put you out there in the icy cold vacuum of airless space. I guess we will find out."

Frantically I put on the spacesuit because I had a gut feeling that Milton was not going to give me much time to suit up. I narrowly got the helmet on when an opening appeared and outer space looked me square in the face. I hesitated, as I am sure a parachutist would on their first jump. However, the little helper would have none of it and shoved me out the hole and into the dark void without a tether!

The only time I remember screaming louder was when my youngest daughter talked me into going on a roller coaster ride with her. Although space was a remarkable sight from the safety of the inside of the ship, it was another story when thrown helplessly out into it. I let Milton know how I felt about it!

"What the fuck, Milton! What are you doing to me? Is this for real? You are going to pick me up, right?"

I flailed my arms and legs in hopeless desperation as I spun speedily into oblivion, while Milton took his sweet time answering me. Meanwhile the little android that shoved me out of the ship mockingly waved goodbye from the opening and continued watching me as I rolled helplessly further away from the ship. I drifted accompanied only by the strained sounds that came from my vocal cords that filled my own ears. Milton had probably tuned me out, which might have been a good thing considering what I had called him. He did ignore my pleas and curses and let me calm down before he responded to me. After what seemed an eternity of drifting further and further from the ship, which had become a distant speck, Milton reassured me that I would be fine.

"Relax, Michael. You are one hundred percent safe. No one is compromised on my watch. I don't think, anyway. I'm giving you a few more minutes out there to enjoy yourself before I bring you back in, so have fun and try to take pleasure in the view that few people will ever have!"

I was somewhat reassured by Milton's words and regained my fragile and battered composure and whatever was left of my dignity, which I would never fully recoup. I completely lost my cool and felt foolish for having panicked so easily.

It was all real. I was floating out in space. There was no way it was a computer projection on a screen. I felt like an idiot. Why had I panicked so quickly? The experience was too fantastic for this rat (me) to comprehend and fully appreciate. I was suspended in space outside of an alien spaceship and looking at planet Earth. I floated like a speck of dust hundreds of miles above Earth—why me? What have I done to be worthy of such mind-blowing adventures?

I drifted and savored my front row view of the universe for an unknown length of time, which may have been about fifteen minutes or an hour. I did not know because my watch stopped working. Had it been working, I had no way of seeing it because it was covered inside the sleeve of the spacesuit. Whatever the length of time, it was not long enough and I was fearful that Milton was going to pull me back in and spoil my fun—for having called him all those nasty things. I drifted a good distance from the ship, perhaps about eight hundred yards or more. The ship had turned into a small dot over the face of the Earth. The immensity of planet Earth hanging there in space like a large Christmas ornament left me beyond awe struck. I had difficulty wrapping my mind around such a view and told Milton that every human on Earth needs to see and experience that miracle! He did not respond.

My space walk ended as abruptly as it began and Milton's ship appeared next to me. The android reached out of the opening in the ship, grabbed me unceremoniously by a strap on the back of the spacesuit, and pulled me in like a piece of space junk.

The android was four-feet-tall or thereabouts, slender, with a little more meat than a stickman and strong as Hercules. Its oval head had no facial features. It had a menacing quality that was unpleasant.

The android helped me out of the spacesuit and then it exited the room, but Not through the door. The android went through the wall, like a ghost, and took the suit and helmet with it.

I was not sure that anything could top the feeling of freedom I had experienced while floating out in space. However, Milton had something else in store for me. I could not imagine what, so I sat down on the theater seat in anticipation of my next treat. The very instant my rear hit the seat the room lights turned off and the screen in front of me lit up. Milton's voice came over the speaker system in the room, instead of telepathically, which was unusual.

"Would you like some popcorn and a soft drink, Michael? Never mind, only joking with you, Michael."

"I'm not hungry, thirsty, or tired. Why is that, Milton? I don't get it. I should have exhausted myself flailing my limbs as I did when the droid tossed me overboard like a piece of trash, and I panicked. Yet I am not perspiring, tired, or hungry, nor in need of a drink. What gives Milton? I always snack back on Earth after much less exertion. Oh, and by the way, thanks for the experience of my life and feel free to throw me out into space anytime!"

"You are welcome and I might just do that. Concerning the quantity of energy you expended during your panic attack: that was minimal. You did burn a few calories while you were out there, but you were not fighting against any forces. There was no gravity, no friction, and no wind, so your energy needs were negligible. Your body also absorbs vital nutrients from the air in this ship and from that spacesuit while you're in it. I could leave you out there for a very long time and the suit would sustain your physical requirements while the view would sustain your spiritual desires. I may go into more detail about that later. For now, sit back, relax, and enjoy the movie, Michael."

The movie started rolling and I was surprised to see that I played a leading role. I was at a shopping mall that was nearest to my house. Supposedly, the incident on the screen took place a few weeks after Christmas of that particular year. I was immediately suspicious of what I saw and kind of blown away because I hardly ever went to that mall except with my wife.

"I don't remember being at the mall without my wife. Are you guys creating stuff about me, Milton?"

"Not creating anything. What you see is what happened. Some things remain blocked from your memory for obvious reasons. Blocked for your protection and peace of mind, Michael, because they do not concern your normal human life and we want to keep your two lives separate. We are opening up some of the hidden memories that are relevant to other things that you will discover today. That is why I'm showing this to you now."

"I'm leading a secret life? What am I, James Bond?"

"James Bond! Don't make me laugh, Michael. My teeth fall out when I laugh."

My on screen personality went to a bookstore at the mall and headed straight for the discount book section where I (he) perused piles of books. That was characteristic of me; I often spent time at bookstores while my wife shopped. My favorite subjects are world history and the people who make history.

While looking through the books, a woman "intentionally" bumped into me and then excused herself, "Oh pardon me." I smiled and gave her a nod. She then noticed the book I was leafing through and made a comment about how she too was interested in historical literature. In the ensuing conversation, I asked her if she would like to get some coffee at one of the shops in the mall. Naturally, that was a come on to explore other interests that had nothing to do with books and favorite authors and that was not characteristic of me.

"What bunk, Milton. My wife would never buy that and neither do I. Are you trying to blackmail me with this phony B movie, Milton? Is that what this charade is all about?"

"Do you always talk during movies, Michael? Anyway, you had a legitimate encounter with that woman. It was strictly business, nothing more. Trust me, your wife will never know unless you tell her, which I highly recommend that you don't."

While chatting with the woman at the coffee shop, I learned that she had several books in her library at home that would interest me. Should I wish to go to her house to see her collection, I was more than welcome to do so. She said it in one of those seductive and inviting voices that few mortal men can resist. She even winked and blew a kiss my way. Startled by her rather bold invitation, I ended up spilling some of my hot coffee on my trousers. Who could blame me? She was one hot-looking babe. Certainly, I was more concerned with her literature back in her apartment and not her sexual innuendoes, wink wink.

"That's not only cheesy, Milton, it is absolute rubbish, I would never cheat on my wife over some floozie no matter how good she looked!"

I was in my early fifties and carried my age well, at least on the screen. The woman was in her early forties and looked half my age. With her foxy body, she could easily have been a model at a top fashion agency. I did not remember ever meeting such a person. I think her personality and her looks would have burned into my memory. Yet, there she was and there I was, salivating over her like a lovesick teenager.

We left the mall together and decided to take her car and leave mine in the parking lot. She had a ruby red Porsche 911 Carrera.

"Michael, we added the Porsche into the movie for effect. She actually rode with you in your car. And you did take her to her apartment."

"So you inserted a car into the scene that was not really there? Well, you obviously did the same with me, because I was not really there, either."

"You were there, Michael. Now hush and watch the rest of the movie."

We get to her place and once we are in her apartment, she offered me a mixed drink. I told her what I liked and she made me a bourbon and Coke. To my surprise, she lied about her library. I did not see a single book in her studio apartment, not even a bookshelf. After she handed me the drink she immediately began to undress in front of me. I sat on the sofa with a goofy childish grin on my face, took a sip from my bourbon and Coke while trying to keep my eyes on her and ended up spilling my drink on my shirt. Completely naked, she walked over to me, took the drink out of my hand and led me to the bed. The bed was next to the couch. She undressed me, and we made love. The screen went blank and the room lights in the ship turned back on.

I sat there on the theater seat shaking my head and chuckling in disbelief. It bothered me the things they can do with props and computer graphics. William Shakespeare was right "All the world is a stage, and we be actors on it," or something to that affect. Obviously some of us actors are not very talented, especially those of us unaware that we are leading a double life.

"It never happened, and if it did I was neither a willing nor an aware participant! If you people, or whatever you are, have concocted my life, then what good is freewill? Assuming there is such a thing as freewill. If I were actually involved certainly, I would remember something as corny and repugnant as what I just saw. Now you got me all confused, Milton! Did I, or did I not, cheat on my wife?"

"You didn't cheat on your wife, Michael. Excluding the Porsche, what you just viewed on the screen took place exactly as you saw it, albeit under our spell. Freewill is real, but you didn't violate it because you were operating under higher orders and unaware of many of your actions."

I was scratching my head trying to figure out how such a chunk of my life could be missing and manipulated without my being the least bit aware of it. I scrutinized my memory from the last few months of my life that supposedly contained the segment I just watched and nothing seemed amiss. There was no room for those shenanigans without removing other segments of my life. Racking my brain proved futile. I could not find any discrepancies and was convinced that it never happened.

While sitting there contemplating what other mind benders Milton had up his sleeve, a naked woman walked through the door and into the room. It was the same woman that was on the screen with me at the bookstore and then at her apartment where we made love. I nearly fell out of my seat! Then she casually spoke to me.

"Hi, Mike, are you up for another round of fun and intrigue like our last encounter?"

I stuttered out the words, "What the hell is going on here?"

"Make love to me, Mike. You know you want to!"

A bed then emerged out of the wall and she came over to where I was sitting, took my hand and led me over to the bed. I was in a state of shock and seemingly helpless as when I was at the park that morning and Milton snared my body and soul with his ship. Seductively, she removed my clothes and we made love as if we were on our honeymoon. I was no match for the sexually enticing powers that radiated from her magical body. She was one gorgeous and dauntingly attractive lovemaking machine.

After she received what she came for, she got up and left the room without saying a word. I remained on the bed somewhat mentally exhausted and puzzled by her abrupt departure.

"That's it? Most women remain in bed and cuddle after sex, unless they are hookers. Milton, is she a hooker? If so, what is her purpose, blackmail?

"She is not human, Michael. She is a biological sperm extractor. There are many ways to get sperm from donors such as you, but this is the most effective way and the best way to retrieve semen. Extracting sperm without proper sexual arousal compromises the quality of the seed and I know you do not want that.

"Sperm extractor? I never signed up to be a sperm donor! Especially with some zombie creature—that is just wrong! Why in hell do you want my sperm anyway? What about my rights in this matter? Don't I have any reproductive say in this highly personal venture?"

"Your body is a container for certain enzymes and other biological products, including sperm. We store and synthesize these items in your body and then extract them at certain intervals when needed. The body you reside in, Michael, is a product of the sperm we extracted from another individual such as yourself before you were even born. Your body is a continuation of this type of container. In essence, your body doesn't belong to you. It belongs to us."

"Who the heck is '*us*'? So, I am an unwitting continuation of some crazy experiment you people are doing here on Earth? You only want me for my body fluids? That is disgusting! I'm going to have to chew on this one for a long while."

"We want you for your mind too, Michael. Your emotions and other factors contribute to the process that binds and mixes these elements inside of you. It is like shaking a bottle of carbonated soda before opening it; we do it for the fizz factor. You are not a continuation of some experiment. Well, not completely. I cannot tell you more at this juncture. I don't want to spoil the surprise."

"If it weren't for the fact that I'm having fun on this ship, and I'm not talking about my romp with the sperm extrapolator, I would be pissed off. Now that I know I had sex with a biological machine, my sex life might be over. This is too much information for me all at once, Milton. Have you considered that? Anyway, so far, most of my experiences on this ship with you have been mind-blowing fantastic. So it's difficult for me to remain upset about anything at this time, including the fact that my body is being used without my knowledge or consent."

4

SUPER STRUCTURE IN
DEEP SPACE

I walked out of the room and went to the corridor with the portholes to try to clear my mind. I looked out the window for some cosmic encouragement and noticed that something was very different. Earth was missing! I ran down the other side of the corridor looking to see if it was there, but what I saw nearly floored me!

The ship was docked to a huge structure with hundreds, if not thousands, of similar ships as the one I was in. The docked ships on the megalithic structure looked like the stubble on my unshaven face every morning. The structure was several thousand feet in each direction and I could not see where the structure began or ended from my vantage point.

"Michael, the portholes are moveable as you learned earlier during your failed escape attempt. Just move one to a spot above you or below you, so that you don't end up straining your neck."

"I can't reach the ceiling, so how do I move a porthole to a spot above me?"

"You are in space where gravity is optional. Give yourself a boost with a little upward push using your toes. The gravity in the ship is equal on the ceiling and walls as it is on the floor. You can walk on the ceiling and walls if you so desire."

I did as Milton suggested and floated to the ceiling and positioned a porthole directly above where I was standing. I then realized that the ceiling now felt like the floor and the floor looked like the ceiling.

"Now I'm totally confused, Milton. Where is up and where is down? And where the hell are we? I don't see Earth anymore. Where is Earth? Just when I think I'm getting accustomed to this crazy stuff and enjoying myself, all the rules change and my mind is forced into higher leaps of strangeness! Where have you taken me, Milton?"

"Making higher mental leaps is progress, Michael. Anyhow, in space there is no up, down, or sideways. We took a little trip while you were watching the movie. We are now a few million miles from Earth and nearer to the star that you humans call the sun. This ship is parked on the dark side of a mother ship, or space station, if you prefer that term."

I was standing on the ceiling and looking down through the porthole rather than looking up. Man I was confused! I saw a gigantic slab that radiated a yellow glow from the structure. The glow was approximately a seven-hundred-foot thick film that projected from the dark slab object. The yellow layer acted to camouflage the structure from Earth and blended perfectly with the backdrop of the sun (according to what Milton told me). The structure itself was pure black. The pixels that made up the glowing skin were spheres about the size of a house and spaced equally apart in a huge matrix type grid. I could see the other ships parked in the gap between the structure and the glowing skin. The gap was about a thousand feet wide and the ships attached to the structure clung to it like strawberry seeds on a strawberry and slightly embedded into the super structure.

I jumped in slow motion to the floor, grabbed hold of a porthole and slid it to the spot below me. As far as my eyes could see, was more of the same super structure. This appeared to be a space station without end and speckled with numerous pod-like ships.

"How big is this thing, Milton? And what the heck is it?"

"It's big enough, and as far as what it is you will find out as much as you need to know shortly. By the way, Michael, the portholes move via telepathy. Give it a try next time you want a better view."

"I was afraid you might say something like that. I am teetering between ecstasy and madness and you keep adding straw to the tired old camel's back. What makes you so sure I can handle all this stuff? I can't even think straight and now you suggest that I can move solid objects with my mind?"

"Don't blow a gasket just yet, Michael. We have quite a ways to go today and I need you to remain mentally intact, if at all possible. Certainly, I am pushing info at you without giving you time to assimilate it via the normal human rate. I need to discover at what rate you can handle new and exotic concepts. That is exactly what we are going to find out, Michael. You must remember one thing; everything is simply information. There is no magic, only perception of magic. For instance, there are people on Earth that have no clue about microwave ovens or how they operate. To them, microwaves are magic. Whereas to others, that magic is a device used for cooking food. Same object, different perceptions. Now go back to that hallway with the doors and look for the green door and enter it."

I walked past several doors, all white, and came to the green one. I hesitated going in because I knew there was probably another mind-blender behind it (and that is not a typo, I really meant "blender"). I took a deep breath, opened the door and walked through it.

What lay before me nearly brought me to tears (again). I had become a maudlin fool during the twists, turns, and the turmoil of endless mind games, not to mention the shear awe of what I experienced that morning. I could not help it. I had seen the face of god and I still lived! I nearly passed out from absolute unadulterated and sinful delight. The sun, as in solar, encompassed a large portion of the view of the monstrously large glassed-in enclosure that was the superstructure. The glass took up the whole front of the massive spaceport, which overflowed with the glow of the sun. Every detail of the sun was visible, yet there was no heat or blinding glare. That was amazing because it was as if we were near the surface of the sun.

The enclosure looked to be several hundred stories high and equally as wide and deep. It appeared to be a perfect cube, but no way for me to tell the size or shape because I could not see the whole structure. Venus was also prominent in the view and was about the size of a grape, but not much more than a pimple on the face of the sun.

"Thank you, Milton! I owe you big time for this one! How can I possibly ever return the favor? Is this what heaven is like? Is this heaven? Have I died and gone to heaven and you are showing be around the place? Is it possible to top this one experience? I can hardly conceive of anything more beautiful. I felt complete. What more could I possibly ask for in life?"

"Hate to burst your bubble, Michael. This is nothing compared to the whole picture and the endless wonders throughout this Milky Way galaxy."

"If that is true, why then are humans kept in the Dark Ages of ignorance about such wondrous things? We believe ourselves to be on the cutting edge of space exploration with our pathetic little probes to Mars, Jupiter, Saturn and the rest of the planets. Yet from what you have shown me in the last hour or so, space has been explored and conquered eons ago. And humans, for the most part, remain ignorant and oblivious to apparently everything."

"Earth is a playpen for some humans and a prison for other humans, Michael. Millions of similar planets such as Earth exist throughout this galaxy. The majority of the people on them have blinders on also, just as humans on Earth do. But on the flip side, there are millions of planets that are utopia-grade and the people and entities on them live blissful, content lives, unencumbered by wars, famine, natural disasters, death, hate and envy."

"What is this thing, this massive structure out in space? What possible purpose could it have so near the sun? And most importantly, who built it?"

"It was built by machines many millions of Earth years ago, for the purpose of entertainment and as a transportation hub."

"Millions of years ago by machines for entertainment and transportation, for whom? Humans have not been on Earth that long. Are you saying there were people on Earth as far back as that?"

"This structure was built for people like you, Michael, and yes there were people on Earth millions of years ago who visited this place, as you are doing now."

"I feel so special, pardon my sarcasm, but why not let the rest of the human population know about this place? And the fact that human types have been on Earth apparently forever. What harm could it do, besides make them start twitching like I'm doing now?"

No answer from Milton.

I was standing on a balcony that overlooked a large open glassed atrium. The balcony was one of hundreds stacked and staggered on top of each other, at approximately thirty-foot intervals. The material of the structure looked metallic and futuristic and not something built or created millions of years ago. The glass facing the sun was one solid piece, one tremendously huge plate-glass window!

The balcony I was on appeared to be hundreds of stories up. Above me, there were several hundred more stories as well. That place was immense!

Additionally, there were large outcroppings on the side facing the glass, each with their unique and grand views of the atrium and the sun. They were docked platforms that could detach and move about the atrium and each had quaint street markets and cafes built onto them. Exotic plants and spectacular varieties of colorful and fragrant flowers adorned the balconies and the platforms. Some of the plants even had ripe fruit dangling from robust branches. Sparkling waterfalls hung in midair and dropped hundreds of feet into floating ponds that drifted around the open atrium like hot air balloons.

"If there ever was a Garden of Eden, it must have looked like this? Am I right, Milton?"

"Gardens of Eden make up the majority of existence in this galaxy, and the countless billions of other galaxies that are chockfull of planetary systems. Edens with every kind of advanced life imaginable and more so, unimaginable, exist throughout the universe."

"Does anything excite you, Milton? You sound so blasé about all this, while I'm running around like a dog in heat, trying to soak in the few morsels you drop off the table, while all around me are banquets fit for the gods."

No answer.

Milton then materialized onto the balcony a few feet from me. It was like a scene out of "Star Trek." He was in his scary-looking alien costume, but I was not fazed like I was the first time I saw him that morning. Then Milton caused a platform to open up around the small balcony we were on and it swallowed the small balcony. The larger platform engulfed the balcony like a larger fish consuming a smaller one and the platform jetted out five hundred feet into the atrium, carrying us out with it. The platform remained attached to the structure or building, or whatever that huge complex was. Bakery-type shops overflowing with pastries and other scrumptious delicacies surrounded the open plaza with a European Renaissance theme, cobblestones and all.

Without the fear factor, Milton's appearance seemed more familiar and natural to me, more so than my human associates back on Earth. I felt as if I had known him for a very long time prior to that morning. However, I could not quite comprehend our relationship because most of it remained blocked in my mind. Once the platform came to a stop, Milton looked at me and telepathically asked me:

"Are you up for a stroll through the market place, Michael?"

"I don't deserve this, Milton. I have done nothing in my life that merits me having this fantastic experience. I almost feel ashamed."

"This has nothing to do with deserving or not deserving something, Michael. This place is here and you are here to learn a few things, nothing more."

"I am learning to love this learning thing of yours, Milton!"

The fresh baked bread and pastries and the delightful aroma of brewed exotic coffees spiced up the air. What was there to learn? These things were for enjoyment, not for pondering over by small human minds like mine. Besides, my mind was basting in the juices of enchantment and I did not want to spoil it by giving myself a "pondering" headache.

Milton walked towards the shops and I followed him like a cheerful puppy, wagging its tail, anticipating more treats. I perused the assortment of decadent delicacies in the market like a child in a candy store. My eyes were bulging and my mouth salivating, while Milton remained nonchalant. What a contrast we made!

The shops were void of people, aliens, and androids, which left that whole platform to Milton and me. All that food just for me, because Milton was not eating any of it. That did not seem right, but who was I to argue? That platform was a personal, cozy, corner of our own little piece of heaven, or mine at least. I took a plate from the stack of plates on the buffet counter, selected a few items and filled my plate. I poured myself a steaming hot cup of coffee and I sat at one of the tables. Milton took nothing and sat opposite me. The opulence was not much different from that of a fancy hotel at a pricy resort, but infinitely bigger and more lavish. Moreover, it boasted a front row seat to the solar system's greatest show, the sun.

"Milton, is this all real? Or are you creating this in my mind?"

"It's all real, and only a small sample of the stuff the universe is filled with. Still, mind over matter is real."

"Can I create this on my own, Milton?"

"'Use the force, Luke.' Actually no, not while you are in human bondage and not until you have moved up the ladder of existence. The thing about 'mind over matter' is that we are not talking 'human mind' over 'cosmic matter,' but cosmic mind over cosmic matter. We can talk more about it at some other time. It really is complicated."

"I assume, because there is food and beverage here, that there are also bathrooms?"

"No bathrooms. The food and drink are mostly for pleasure with some nutritional value, but zero residuals or waste. Everything you eat and drink here will dissolve completely in your system."

"Bathrooms have other functions than bodily plumbing, Milton. We humans use them to freshen up, like splash water on our faces, wash our hands before we eat, comb our hair, straighten our tie, and tuck our shirts in. And we can look in the mirror to make sure something isn't stuck between our teeth after we eat."

"There is no need for vanity and freshening-up for people in our possession. And should you get something stuck in your teeth, Michael, you can be sure I will tell you about it because that just grosses me out!"

"Maybe you should be a comedian, Milton. Ha Ha. I saw what appeared to be thousands of similar craft like the one we rode in. Ships docked to the face of this colossus of a structure, are they also carrying human cargo for the same reason you are? Which by the way, I remain clueless to what that might be."

"About thirty percent of those vehicles carry human cargo from Earth to this place. The rest are a mixture of hybrids, humans and other life forms from Earth and other planets, moons, and space cities, which are scattered throughout this solar system. There are also some intergalactic beings here as well"

"Why don't I hear or see others on this platform or in this place? Where are they all hiding? Are we alone on this platform? Or are they invisible to me?

"Platforms like this one are personal and private and harbor no other entities, whether they are invisible or not. However, there is an area, a town, inside this structure, where humans and other entities mingle. Would you like to go there now, Michael?"

Without me having said a word, the platform we were on separated from its moorings, dropped several stories and then joined with a larger platform, fitting into it like a missing piece of a puzzle. Our platform with its shops incorporated seamlessly into the larger structure and became one with the larger plaza. People were walking on the cobblestone streets, peering into shop windows, sitting at tables, talking, eating and drinking, as if they were at a typical Earth mall. The setting was similar to any number of shopping districts in large cosmopolitan cities. The exception was the unmistakable contrast of entities such as Milton and freakish looking hybrids, also milling about the place.

I had quit speaking verbally to Milton sometime after we entered into that super structure because I felt like I was talking to myself and became self-conscious about doing it. I noticed that none of the other humans on the plaza verbalized their conversations in the public areas and therefore, I was justified in keeping my mouth shut.

The universe doesn't always abide by human concepts or fundamental laws such as physics.

5

SHOPPING DISTRICT

Milton and I remained seated while I took in the scenery from our table. I was not sure what was next on Milton's list and in no hurry to find out, I was enjoying just sitting there. A few moments went by and one of the aliens in the vicinity made his way over to our table. He looked similar to Milton and appeared to be conversing with Milton telepathically. They looked at each other as if they were communicating. Since I was not privy to their mental discussion, I decided to take that opportunity and strolled over to the shops for some window browsing and to see what alien wonders were for sale.

I walked by a storefront with watches and timepieces that were prominently displayed in the window. Since mine was not working, I decided to inquire about timepieces that might function properly inside alien ships. I entered the store and looked around. For an instant, I forgot that I was a million miles from Earth in some space mall and not back on Earth. The store was similar in many details to human shops, with the exception that everything was free (according to a sign in the store). I picked up a watch that was on a display rack on top of the counter. The attendant approached and asked if she could assist me. She, or it, was a human-looking android that vocalized her speech exactly as we humans do. When she spoke audibly to me, I was thrown off because I was just getting the hang of keeping my mouth shut. Plus, she was a machine and speaking to a machine was creepy. I knew she was an android from the nametag on her lapel identifying her as one. Otherwise, she looked, acted and talked exactly like a woman on Earth. Eerily, the android knew my name and addressed me as any sales person on Earth would have.

"Mike, these watches tell the time of any place within this system of planets and moons. Or if you wish to know the time for any specific area or particular time zone on Earth, we have that too."

Talking with a machine was strange and I felt awkward listening to her describe the watches to me. Stranger still was having to respond to that mechanical being. But then again, she was very real in her demeanor and she was likeable.

"I'll take one that is set for USA Central time zone, please."

She retrieved a watch that fit my specification from a cabinet under the counter and gave me a brief explanation about how it functioned. She then strapped the watch onto my wrist. The watch told me the time in my city back home and the temperature of my present location. It was seventy-eight degrees Fahrenheit in that place. It had other gizmos on it, but she did not explain them sufficiently and I do not recall what they were for or did. Perhaps the watch monitored blood pressure and anxiety levels, but I did not ask her.

"The watch is biodegradable and dissolves rapidly once you exit the ship and it detects Earth's atmospheric pressure."

"That sucks! I was hoping for a souvenir," I told her.

"Will that be all, Mike?

"Yes, thank you."

I departed the shop with my new "space-alien" watch, shaking my head in disbelief that this could all be happening. Yet, it felt more real than my normal life back on Earth. I was in a state of awareness that bordered on the supernatural. Everything was exquisitely clear in my perceptions of things around me. All I was experiencing surpassed my wildest dreams and fantasies. My understanding of life in the universe changed dramatically. I was unwittingly cultivating higher expectations with each new experience and perhaps setting myself up for disappointment. No matter, life on Earth after this was going to be very dull in comparison!

I looked at the watch and noticed that only two hours had passed since the beginning of my adventure that morning. I was flabbergasted. I certainly believed more time had gone by due to all the things I had experienced, events that individually could easily enhance a whole lifetime. That was especially true if one were to compare them to the lukewarm existence most of us humans on Earth endure during our entire lives.

I did not realize it then, but my obsession with time was one of the few downers I had during that fantastic voyage. Time is everything on

Earth. We set our lives by our clocks. Being with Milton, time was irrelevant, as if it did not exist at all. That was a very liberating concept, which unfortunately I was unable to grasp and enjoy in my time-based mindset. Naturally, I could not avoid time. I had a life and family back on Earth and time was certainly important in our lives.

I walked further into the shopping district with a big smile on my face. Time seemed to be on my side, even though I was never sure what time it was. Even with my new watch, how could I know if it was telling me the correct time? I was inside a fantastic alien outpost and it certainly could not get better than that, regardless of what time it was! The sun was shining brightly as it had for billions of years and it did so with never a cloudy overcast to hide behind.

Humans were milling around in the streets and in the shops, but I was hesitant to stop and talk with any of them. Apparently, they too had the same reluctance because everyone walked pass me without saying a word. It did not help that I did not know if the others were from Earth and shared a common language. I decided to try talking anyway and looked for an opportunity to break the ice with someone. I headed towards a fountain that had seating around it. A woman was sitting on one of the benches reading a book. I walked up to her and asked if I could sit on the bench next to her. She looked up at me and spoke a language I never heard before. It did not sound as if it were from Earth. I made a gesture that I did not understand her and walked away feeling a bit uncomfortable. Undeterred, I went up a little ways, approached a man walking towards me on the street and asked him what he thought of this place. He also spoke that same strange language that the woman spoke.

That put a damper on an otherwise upbeat morning. Not being able to communicate with other humans made me feel nauseous and out of place. I was the alien in an alien environment. Being able to corroborate the experience with other humans would have been the icing on the cake, but it did not happen and I complained to Milton.

"Milton, what's the deal? Are there no humans in this place that speak the same language that I do?"

"Sure there are. The two people you spoke to are human and they speak perfect English."

"But they didn't speak English. They spoke a very strange language that sounded alien. It had a squeaky metallic tone to it, which is not a normal human-type speech pattern I've ever heard before."

"Oh, I forgot to tell you, communication with other humans is not allowed. We do not want anyone to corroborate each other's stories and experiences. Extraterrestrials don't exist in the minds of the vast majority of humanity, and we prefer to keep it that way."

"Why do you and your cohorts prefer to keep it that way, Milton?"

"All of the usual stuff: the premature collapse of religious institutions, the loss of faith in the government's ability to protect the people and a meltdown in the financial markets throughout the world. Nations would de-stabilize and anarchy would ensue. It could get messy and then we would have to clean up the mess."

"Don't you think that I'm taking this fairly well? So, why wouldn't others be able to handle it also?"

"You have been in the program for a long time and are conditioned to us somewhat. Even though you only remember a fraction of your past encounters with us, since we blocked most of them out, those interactions with us are still a part of what you are, subconsciously speaking. Today we are going to unblock more of your past association with us and give you new material to upload into your mind."

"How many people on Earth are in the same situation as I am, Milton?"

"We don't like giving those numbers out, Michael."

"How long have you people—do I call you "people?" How long have you people been on Earth?"

"We are not people, as I told you before. We do not procreate as humans and other similar entities in this galaxy. We have been on Earth for what seems forever. And will remain on Earth until the end of the solar system, many millions of years down the road."

"How old are you Milton? And do you have a home planet?"

"At the level I am, we don't age at all. We are pure energy that inhabits various bodies (machines) for the sole purpose of interaction with physical forms such as you, Michael. We do not have one home planet. We operate on many planets and on many dimensional levels."

"Are you a god?"

"You asked that already. No, I am not a god. I have a job. There are many levels of beings like myself. I'm at the mid-range level and working my way up."

"Does this structure, this building, or whatever it is, serve a purpose other that to make someone such as myself feel insignificant in comparison to its awesomeness?"

"It also functions like a Grand Central Station. From this place, you can travel to any of the planets and moons where we have outposts. Are you ready to take a ride to one of those other outposts, Michael?"

"Hell yes! Can I take a camera with me?"

"Certainly! Just pick one up at the camera shop, the one you just passed."

I entered the camera shop, looked around and saw hundreds of cameras and other devices that were foreign to me. Some of the cameras looked exactly like the ones we have on Earth. The attendant in the store approached me and asked if I were looking for any particular camera.

"Which photographic device, camera or camcorder would you recommend for my situation? And do they use memory sticks like cameras on Earth?"

"For Earthlings, I would recommend these cameras over here. They do not need memory sticks or batteries. Take as many pictures or videos as you like. They have unlimited storage capacity."

"So the cameras we get depend on where we come from? Why is that?"

"Some people, entities, can keep their pictures and movies and show them to their families, friends or associates, back on their home planets. Others cannot. Earth is on the blackout list. You can take photos, but you can't bring them back to Earth with you. Photos must remain in your locker."

"I have a locker!"

"Milton will show you your locker before you leave on your trip."

The android handed me the compact camera. I walked out of the store excited about my locker and what marvels could be stored there. After I left the shop, I realized I was no longer in the shopping district from where I had entered the camera store. I was in a completely different area filled with rows of lockers. Somehow, I was transported there instantly.

HALL OF LOCKERS

I was dumbfounded about how I got to the locker "stadium" so quickly, after walking out of the camera shop. What had happened to the platform and the shopping district? I was in a cavernous hall filled with locker-doors as far as the eye could see. That spaceport was huge.

"Milton, did you teleport me to another place as I walked out of the camera shop?"

"Kind of. There were two doors. One was next to the door you entered off the street. As you made your exit from the store, I steered you through that other door. It took you to the locker room where you are now. Did you think I beamed you there, Michael? Don't be silly! I did save you a few steps, however. Now, walk to the door that is glowing. It has your name on it and only you can enter your locker."

I walked to the glowing door that was about a hundred feet from where I came out of the camera shop. I stopped in front of the door. Sure enough, it had my name on it. I felt so special. I also noticed that I was the only one in the entire enormous stadium of lockers. Literally thousands of locker doors covered the walls in every direction of that large hall.

"Am I the only person here, Milton?"

"No, there are others further down the hall, too far for you to see from where you are. And there are many inside their lockers as we speak."

"Inside their lockers? Why would people be inside their lockers, Milton? Can they get out of their lockers? You are not going to lock me inside a locker and leave me there, Milton, are you?"

"What if I did? Do you think you have any control of what I do, or can do, with you, Michael?"

"Am I only a mouse to you, Milton? Am I only a toy to play with?"

"Ever catch a mouse, Michael? Not easy! Mice are fast little critters and usually get away. You are not a mouse, and you can't get away."

"What happened to free will and human rights? My rights? Don't I have any?"

"You left those cushy ideals and illusions back on planet Earth, Michael."

"Why are you wasting your time with someone like me who has little importance, Milton? I have no power, no rights, and presumably no value?"

"You have value, immense value, otherwise you wouldn't be here. Most people on Earth have value. Power and rights are human illusions and no one on Earth really has either of them. Now quit stalling and enter your locker, Michael."

The door stopped glowing and it opened. I entered and the door closed behind me. The locker was not a locker, but a room about fifteen feet by fifteen feet, very large for a locker. My idea of a locker was a school locker. This was like a storage garage. At the center of the room was a metal table. On the table were a dozen wooden boxes of various sizes, all of them smaller than a shoebox and scattered around the table. The boxes looked like the ones I made in woodshop back in grade school--nothing fancy, but they did have sentimental value and memories from my past.

I walked to the table and opened up one of the boxes. The box had an assortment of rocks and strange objects that looked like items a child would collect. Pictures were in the box, pictures of a planet taken from one of its moons by a young boy (me) many years ago.

"I remember collecting these items when I was about ten-years-old, Milton. I did not know the name of the planet at the time, but I recognize it now from the pictures as Uranus. From which moon did I take these pictures, Milton?"

"The moon is called Miranda on Earth. We have bases on all the Uranus moons and you visited a couple of them. Those rocks and items in your boxes are from different moons in orbit around Uranus and some other planets. Would you like to visit Uranus now?"

"We're not talking anal probe are we, Milton?"

"Before we make the space jump, its better not to have anything in your system, so yes. But that has nothing to do with the planet. You humans named it. The probe is painless and if you wish, it can be blocked from your memory."

"Please block it from my memory, Milton."

Reality is merely an illusion,
albeit a very persistent one.

Albert Einstein

6

SPACE GATE URANUS

Instantly I find myself in another part of the space station, away from my locker. Milton blocked out whatever he or his assistants did to prep me for my journey to Uranus. I was disappointed because I was eager to look inside some of the other boxes before leaving, but I did not get the chance. There was no way of knowing when, if ever, I would get another opportunity to explore those boxes. The idea that the boxes contained things from other worlds was tormenting me with curiosity. Opening the one box jarred loose many memories of my childhood and how I was involved in the space program during my early years. I was left with more questions that Milton did not seem eager to answer. When I closed the box, only pertinent information that would serve me during that day remained with me. The rest melted away. I could only imagine the memories locked away inside those other boxes.

I was back in the main gallery of the super structure with all the shops, but presumably at one of the other ends. The magnificent sun remained prominently in view and the sight of it continued to strike awe in my soul. One look into the sun and my soul filled with indescribable joy. There is certainly much more to the sun than we humans understand, but that mystery remained hidden in Milton's bag of tricky knowledge and he didn't tell me what that magic was. Milton did promise to drop some hints about the sun and its supernatural properties on a future visit.

Large crowds of people lined up towards the front of the glassed area facing the sun. There were many gates to the different planets and other mysterious destinations. Each gate had long lines that added intrigue and excitement to the whole affair.

Milton told me to get in the first line I reached. Large ships docked to the glass of the structure and people streamed into them like a trail of ants a mile long. No one was carrying luggage, purses, or backpacks. Each person had only the clothing they were wearing. Hundreds of huge ships were crowded into a small corner of the immense glass structure. From where I stood, the ships looked like short filaments of fat spaghetti attached to the outside of the glass, like stubble.

The serpentine lines of people moved quickly across huge platforms, forming bridges spanning the large open space of the atrium like capillaries of a river delta, pouring streams of people into the harbor and into the open mouths of gigantic ships. The view during the walk towards the ships elicited the full spectrum of human emotions. I noticed many people in my line wiping tears from their eyes as they marveled at the incredible panorama in front of us. I was equally mesmerized and filled with overwhelming emotion. Tears of joy ended up blurring my view of the cosmic splendor before us. Some people stepped out of the line and got down on their knees as if they were praying. Perhaps some were simply over-stimulated with elation and paused for a moment.

Everyone appeared to be traveling alone, without family or friends to share the experience. I wished that I had my family with me on this soul-expanding journey. No young children or anyone that looked under the age of eighteen was in my line, but I could see there were children in some of the other lines. It appeared that the ratio of women and men was even. Some people were very old, perhaps in their nineties, but all looked like they were in good health. Everyone in my line was able to walk without devices and help from others.

"Milton, you seem to be with me no matter where I am? Are you going on this trip? If not, will we remain in communications as we are now?"

"I'm not going on the Uranus trip. I will be in the vicinity of Saturn. Nevertheless, you and I will be in contact as we are now for the most part. Distance has no relevance on the mind-wave, which I will use to keep in contact with you."

The ship grew from the sliver I could see when I first got in line to a cylindrical monstrosity as I neared the point of entry. The thing was a tanker more than a hundred stories high and twice as long. It was charcoal black and nearly invisible in dark space. With the solar backdrop, the ship had an ominous and overwhelmingly eerie presence.

The container was intimidating and tantalizing, all rolled up into one strange mind-boggling sensation.

There were much larger vehicles along the glass structure that seriously dwarfed the one I was about to enter. I could only imagine what marvelous destinations awaited those entering such gigantic ships. Milton only commented about things that concerned me, so I could only speculate about others and their destinations.

We entered the cylinder ship at the very center of its pancake-flat facade. The ship attached to the glass structure like a suckerfish stuck to the inside of an aquarium. While standing directly in front of the cylinder, one only sees a large, black, disk with no markings on it. The platform that led up to the entrance was transparent and perfectly centered to the cylinder's entrance. The ramp's design allowed for the full view of the cylinder's face, so its full spectrum from top to bottom could be seen.

The line of people moved quickly into the cylinder's disk. Once inside, I walked into what looked like a huge, rotating honeycomb. The whole ship consisted of small, one-person compartments running the length of the ship. Many rows of compartments were stacked on top of each other like racks inside a bakery oven. The interior of the cylinder ship rotated slowly without coming to a full stop. The rotation was like a Ferris wheel with hundreds of slots on each level. I stepped into one of the compartments. It locked shut, sealing me inside.

I was not the least apprehensive about being inside a strange cocoon that was about to shoot towards the periphery of our solar system nearly two billion miles away. What was wrong with that picture? I asked myself. I had always been claustrophobic, or so I thought, but that cramped little space did not bother me. Perhaps Milton sedated me when I was prepped for the journey. I did not feel sedated.

I hadn't the faintest understanding of what I might be in for during that trip. I might as well been jumping into an active volcano for all I knew. What I would do when I got to that frozen gas giant of a planet was beyond my comprehension. I did not care. I wanted to go and felt blessed that I had that opportunity.

Milton didn't bother telling me details about that journey. Milton did not say how long the trip would take or why I was going to such a faraway planet in the first place. Nor did he explain to me why the other people were going there. I asked Milton all these questions, but he didn't respond. I looked at my watch and noted that I was into this crazy and wondrous adventure about three hours and with no idea when it was due to end, not that I wanted it to end.

I was able to stand upright in the compartment, but not for long. A metallic platform rose out of the floor about two feet and stopped. As it came up through the floor, I was forced to sit down on the platform. About then, Milton chimed in and told me to lie down and not to worry about what was going to happen. "It is painless and safe," he said.

"Can you see me, Milton?"

"Yes, I monitor your thoughts and visuals. I see what your eyes see and what your mind thinks or perceives about its surroundings."

The air was sucked out of my compartment, which was then rapidly filled with a gel-like substance. As the gel filled the compartment, I lost consciousness. Yet, I remained in a state of suspended, unexplainable awareness. My consciousness was not inside the compartment or inside my head. I could see the compartment and my body as if I were hovering outside of it and above it. Somehow, I was detached from my body.

PLANET URANUS

The cylinder craft docked to a large, dark, slab similar to the spaceport in orbit around the sun from which I had departed. Other cylinder ships of various sizes also docked at numerous places on four sides of the vertical totem pole like spaceport. I saw that even while my dormant body remained encased in foam inside the cylinder.

Seconds after the ship docked the gel or foam in my cubical absorbed back into the walls and I instantly regained full consciousness. I sat up and the compartment door opened. I exited the compartment and felt no fatigue or drowsiness. I also did not feel any effects from the flight or from the foamy material that I was encased in on the way to Uranus. There was no residue or wetness from the foam on me or on my clothing. I walked out of the chamber as dry as when I entered. I had no memory of the trip. However, I was fully aware of myself and able to see things around me during the flight. The trip itself seemed instantaneous.

I followed the others as they emerged from their compartments and filed out of the ship in orderly lines, as if it had been rehearsed a hundred times. The people all looked as if they simply were stepping out of a subway train or bus and making their way to work. No one talked as we disembarked from that huge monstrosity of a vehicle, but some smiled at me as we headed to the exit. We entered into a large, glass-enclosed gallery that faced Uranus. I remembered the planet from my first visit out there as a child. It did not have the same impact on me back then as it did this time. I nearly fell over from the sight of the peculiar-looking planet.

Two or three, perhaps more, of the travelers fainted shortly after entering the gallery from the ship. Presumably, those that collapsed were overwhelmed by the awesome sight of the planet and not from the effects of the flight up there in tight quarters. They were helped by some of the other passengers, recovered immediately, and then were awed with the rest of us.

I was dumbfounded and mesmerized by the sight of Uranus and could not take my eyes away. Uranus was surreal. Then there was the shock of realizing that we were over a billion miles from Earth. Here we were, looking at one the furthest planets from the sun, at the friggin' edge of the solar system! Who would believe it? I was there and I could not wrap my little mind around that fact.

Astoundingly, the whole trip took less time than an airplane flight from St. Louis, Missouri, to Huston, Texas. Incomprehensible it was and is!

"Milton, how did we travel here so quickly? We are talking faster than light speed! That is impossible and illogical, according to our human physics. It simply does not compute!"

"Impossible for the human-grade, 21st century technological point of view. Yes, it certainly is! However, we use technology that is thousands of years ahead of what is available to humans on Earth. Light speed is not a factor in our mode of travel anymore than the stagecoach is a factor in taking people on international airline flights across Earth's oceans. How many people and scientists belonging to the stagecoach era would have believed it possible that huge jetliners would carry 500 people and be able to cross the oceans in a few hours? The same number as today's human scientists who also could never be convinced that planetary travel in a few hours is not only feasible, but a reality throughout the Milky Way galaxy of star systems."

CLOAK AND DAGGER

The rings around Uranus were tilted perpendicular to the planet as we viewed them from the galleria. Uranus looked like a huge ball going through a multi-ringed and colorful hoop. The hue of the rings had a faint rainbow shade as they reflected electromagnetic waves from the faint sun. I and the other people in the lobby were mesmerized by the planetary spectacle of moons, rings and the mystical aura that shrouded Uranus.

It soon became apparent that not all who disembarked from our ship were there as tourists. The non-tourist stuck out from the crowd mainly due to their somber appearances and lack of enthusiasm that had enraptured the rest of us. Few seemed to take notice of this vagabond cadre of souls that mingled in the crowd, but for some strange reason, I did. These dismal people looked as if they did not want to be there at all and that puzzled me. It soon became apparent why they looked apprehensive and disenfranchised. The non-tourist knew something that the rest of the tourist did not.

From seemingly out of nowhere, dozens of three-foot-tall, gray-skinned alien creatures, possibly androids, fanned out into the recently arrived crowd that I was part of and began randomly harvesting people from it, mostly those gloomy-looking people.

"Don't be alarmed, Michael, not everyone is there for the same reasons that you and the other tourists are there. Some of the humans you traveled with are under a sentence of sorts and are being culled."

The androids emerged from the crowd each holding a person by the wrist and leading them out of the crowd and towards a bank of elevators. The people led away did not look overly alarmed, as if they understood what was going on and had expected to be taken. There was no sign of anyone attempting to run away from the short alien critters who were presumably acting as the police force. The rest of the crowd did not seem bothered by the subtle display of authoritarianism that took place under our noses, which I thought strange. It was as if everyone there received reassurance by his or her own Milton-type entities as I did. I was disturbed by what I saw. The subtle but aggressive nature of the alien critters put a damper on the otherwise fabulous experience.

After Milton told me not to worry, I tried not to let what I witnessed distract me and continued to enjoy the wonders of Uranus and its intriguing moons. That trip certainly seemed a promising odyssey and I did not want anything to mess it up. Nevertheless, messed up it did get.

That odyssey took a nasty turn, which I had not foreseen, especially after Milton's reassurance. As I was making my way to get a better look from an observation deck on another level, a cold hand reached up behind me and clasped around my left arm. I turned to see who had the audacity to accost me in such a rude and forceful manner. One of those little gray creatures clenched my arm, led me out of the crowd, and took me away with the other criminals. I was in near panic!

"Milton, what is happening? Why are they taking me?"

"Remain calm, Michael. I will need to investigate what has caused this mix-up."

I tried to break free by pulling my arm away from that thing, but could not budge my arm. The small, alien creature had a grip like a vice and the strength of the Hulk, incredible power for a creature the size of a nine-year-old child. That explained why the non-tourist did not bother struggling and passively went with the androids; they understood the futility of trying to escape from those critters.

The rest of the people remained unconcerned that a brigade of alien enforcers took some of us to some other sinister location. The oblivious people continued to explore the space station without me. I was so pissed off! I was cheated out of a fabulous vacation because of some stupid alien bureaucratic blunder!

Meanwhile, I and the other undesirables were taken to a lower level of the space station in a freight elevator, which all of us were placed into like sardines. My claustrophobia was back! Luckily, the elevator ride was short and they loaded about sixty of us into a spacious shuttle awaiting us on that level. I saw no females in the bunch of inmates. All were human males, at least in outward appearance. I believe I was the senior, the oldest one among them. The others looked to be in their twenties, thirties, and forties.

"Milton, where are they taking me?"

No answer.

For the first time since my encounter with Milton that morning, I felt truly alone. All the pleasure of the previous moments quickly turned to despair. It was not as if I were lost in some city back on Earth where I could eventually find a way out of my situation. I was millions of miles from Earth without a clue or lifeline except Milton, and he seemed to be in a jam himself.

The shuttle I was loaded onto was round and about forty feet in diameter with large floor-to-ceiling windows. The interior glowed brightly and the whole ship was one large, open, spherical room. There was no sign of what powered the shuttle. The shuttle had no visible controls and no cockpit--only a ceiling and a floor that sandwiched a glass exterior wall between them. The shuttle lacked seating or any other stabilizing devices such as hold bars and poles like on subways and buses on Earth.

The androids did not accompany us into the shuttle, which I thought odd. They simply escorted us to the craft, loaded us into it and then went away, probably to menace some other unsuspecting humans that were arriving on other transports. I was the last to enter the shuttle and then the opening closed behind me. After the door closed, I kicked at the door and fell to the floor of the craft, as I did on Milton's ship earlier that morning. Apparently, that "prisoner" craft was made of the same tough, rubbery material as Milton's ship.

I yelled at the top of my voice, "Does anyone speak English?"

No one answered. However, a few did look in my direction momentarily as if they were annoyed by my futile and childish tantrum. Most of the men kept their gaze on the planet that was prominent in the windows. Others milled around the ship as if they were contemplating their fate. None of them spoke a word the whole time, not to me or to each other.

The shuttle detached from the station minutes after we boarded. There were no public announcements or indications that it was going to depart. The shuttle simply broke away and appeared to freefall towards the planet Uranus, dropping hundreds of kilometers at dizzying speeds.

After a few minutes of freefall towards Uranus in a haphazard fashion, the shuttle stabilized itself. It then shot straight into the planet at a velocity that should have plastered us passengers to the opposite wall. Yet, no one seemed affected by gravitational forces in any way during the freefall, or after it picked up speed. The shuttle traveled several hundreds of miles per hour as if it were a rocket on steroids. That was only my unscientific guess since there was no way for me to know how fast we were traveling.

All I can say about human technology is, "what technology?" Our human technology remains in the Stone Age compared to what is going on in some parts of our solar system.

The ship pierced the atmosphere without signs of any friction. No flames from heat build up splashed across the windows, as one might expect when entering a thick atmosphere. I am not a physicist, but I know that matter coming against matter at those velocities creates friction and tremendous heat. That's why meteors hit Earth's atmosphere, become shooting stars, and burn up before touching the ground. That ship acted like a supernatural cocoon that somehow insulated matter against the effects of other matter, or so it seemed to me.

The atmosphere of Uranus was a blue-greenish shade, but as we penetrated the cloud cover, the colors became brighter and with many hues of orange and red streaks. Colors were amplified by the speed, and mixed with the reflections of the sparse sunlight that was reaching the planet. I looked in the direction of the sun and could see a faint, yet brilliant, light that was shrouded in a crown of white hazy gases.

Below the frosty clouds of Uranus, the ship approached a solid barrier that presumably enveloped the cities below it. The barrier looked metallic and seemed to cover a huge patch above the planet. The speed of the ship made it difficult to judge distance and size, but it covered a significant area above the land. That assumes there was land somewhere near the center of the planet. The structure looked like an upturned cup.

According to my watch, only a few minutes passed from the time we boarded the shuttle to its destination, somewhere inside of the city's enclosure. The ship flew through the metallic-looking enclosure without stopping or slowing down, piercing it like a needle going through fabric. I was certain that we were going to crash into the structure, but I was the only one who showed concern.

Once inside the super structure, the ship attached itself to one of the outer walls surrounding the city. The outer barrier that had looked metallic now looked glass-like on the interior side. The glass covering magnified the sunlight. I deduced that because the sun looked much brighter from the inside of that place than it did while we were in orbit around the planet.

The door of the shuttle opened and revealed a massive lobby that was similar to our busy airports back on Earth. The convicts filed out of the shuttle unescorted. Presumably, they knew where to report, but I sure did not. I was the last to exit the shuttle, not sure that I should. My desire for adventure had waned considerably due to my uncertain circumstances.

The men disappeared into the crowds of human and alien beings, which scurried about the place like hordes of shoppers during Christmas rush. Some of the people could easily have passed for humans, like those that were in the shuttle with me. Others were distinctly different, perhaps hybrids of some kind. Few were more than six feet tall. The majority were about five feet tall, more or less.

The lobby was huge with many levels and platforms like those in the spaceport near the sun. We were dropped off at the uppermost level of that building, which was enclosed under a large glass canopy hundreds of meters wide. The view from there was spectacular and many stars were visible and prominent in the twilight Uranus sky.

I walked around in the large open area like a lost child in a strange land. For the first time since that morning, I felt hungry and thirsty but with nowhere to turn and no idea where to go for answers to my unusual circumstances. I had a light breakfast before I headed to the park for my walk and normally I would snack on something before lunch. That day I didn't snack or eat lunch. The food in the spaceport did not count because it was not real food, according to Milton.

I followed my nose, hoping to pick up a scent of some type of food market, presuming that the alien critters running around the place consumed something similar to what humans eat. My nose did not detect anything at all. However, there was an area that looked like it could be a food court and I walked in that direction.

There were tables and chairs and people type entities putting things into their mouths. People or whatever they were, were sitting around tables and eating just as they do on Earth. I thought I had hit the jackpot until I realized that I had no money and I doubted they took Visa or Master card. Whether or not the food was edible for humans like me did not concern me at that time. I was willing to chance it if I could get some food.

It turned out that money was the least of my problems. Before I reached the food area, I felt the firm and unmistakable grip of an android clasping its hand around my arm. One of those short alien creatures came and took me away from the food court. It was crazy frightening how those bastards snuck up on me without my ever seeing them coming.

The creature swiftly led me out of that area as if I were a leper escaped from a leper colony. I had to walk fast to keep from being dragged across the floor like a ragdoll by the swiftly moving creature. The alien took me to a room not far from where I disembarked from the shuttle moments earlier. The creature put me in a room and left me there.

I never felt as alone as I did then. The door had no handles or doorknobs and I was a prisoner in that room. At one end of the small room, there was a table and some chairs around the table. I sat in one of the chairs and rested my head down on my arm, mentally exhausted by my strange dilemma.

Moments passed and a human-looking man came through the door and immediately began interrogating me. I peeked up at him with one eye open while my head remained rested on my arm. I showed little enthusiasm for his presence. Then it hit me that he was speaking perfect English. He was aggravated with me for some reason and demanded that I sit up and listen to him.

"Who are you and why are you here?" he demanded to know. "And how did you manage to get into this city? You are not allowed in this city!"

I was excited that at last, somebody I could communicate with existed and I did not care if it was the Gestapo! I stood up from the table as he had asked and gave him an answer.

"An alien named Milton sent me here."

"Who or what is Milton?"

"Milton is an extraterrestrial I met this morning on Earth. He put me on a ship to this planet. The ship docked to a space station orbiting Uranus. After disembarking from the ship, the same type of creature that brought me to this room grabbed me and put me into a shuttle that came here."

"So you are here by some freak accident? Is that what you are saying? A breach of that kind is rare and nearly impossible! Someone or something wanted you here and let you slip through our normally impenetrable security."

"I'm hungry. May I please have something to eat and drink? And if I should need to relieve myself, where do I go? I presume you have bathrooms here?"

"There are humans on this planet, but few in this city. Humans who are in this city remain under quarantine and are placed on special diets. Human digestive systems are quite different from ours. You humans have bacteria in your intestines that we do not tolerate. I do have some wafers and a special drink that you can consume and will have a droid bring you some after I am through questioning you. The wafers produce no residuals in your system, but they will give you energy. However, there are no bathroom facilities in this city that you are allowed to use."

"How long will I be kept under quarantine?"

"Until you leave. This will happen when we receive authorization and instructions about what to do with you. There are reading materials with pictures or you can view our version of television. The controls are on the table with the reading materials."

The interrogator left the room the very moment that he stopped talking. As he left, an android entered the room, handed me two wafers and a small container of liquid, and then left. The wafers were the size of a saltine cracker and the liquid might have filled four thimbles, yet they did the trick and I was not hungry or thirsty after I consumed them.

I felt like a prisoner and I looked for something that would take my mind off my insidious predicament. I picked up the television control and it triggered a calamity of sound and visuals that permeated from all the surfaces of that room. The four walls, the ceiling and floor lit up like a three-dimensional television on steroids, literally engulfing me in strange sounds and mind-numbing visuals. Several programs ran simultaneously and cycled yet through dozens of other programs, or so it seemed to my human brain. The room became a mass of confusion as wave after wave of super-sized, lifelike media saturated my ill-equipped mind. I tossed the control back on the table as if it were a wand from hell. Mercifully, everything turned off and the room was back to normal. I was at the end of my wits and did not need that kind of shockwave bombardment. I sat back down at the table and laid my head down. Then Milton chimed in, "Hello, Michael."

I jumped back to life and walked around the table with renewed energy, glad as hell to here his voice.

"Where the hell have you been, Milton? I am ecstatic to hear your voice! Did you fix the screw up so that I can get the heck out of this prison and possibly back to enjoying my stay here? Assuming that remains an option? Or you can take me home, for that matter."

"There was no screw up. It was intentional. I wanted you to get a glimpse of other civilizations in this solar system, so I directed one of the androids to take you to the shuttle. You are a stowaway, as I am sure you know by now. They do not like us doing those things, but they tolerate it. You do not pose a danger to them because we sealed your digestive track before placing you into the transport to Uranus."

"That would have been really wonderful to know, Milton! It might have saved me some mental anguish. Do you have any idea what I have gone through? Anyway, I'm definitely fascinated by this place. Their society seems similar to what we have on Earth except technologically they appear many decades ahead of humans."

"They are much more advanced than Earth—not even in the same classification as Earth. They absorb information rapidly, and they enjoy their lives tremendously, which is unlike Earth where people mostly endure their lives. You got a hint of how quickly they absorb information when you turned on their television device, which is normal entertainment for them. They breathe air similar to humans, but consume food that does not produce waste. They eat and drink small amounts of food compared to humans. They do not get sick because they do not have the same internal organs as humans. Therefore, they remain physically and mentally healthy their entire existence. That is why they get touchy when we sneak a human into their midst, which could cause an imbalance in their complex biological system. But we are a step ahead of them and you don't present any danger to the city."

"Tell me more about them, Milton, if you don't mind."

"The city you are in is a stable society. It did not get that way over time. It was designed that way from the start. The city is not going to advance or decline. It will remain stable for millions of Earth years. The population of that city is one hundred million or so, not including androids and visitors who are legal and illegal such as you. Now, turn the television on and I will find a station for you and mute the rest."

I picked up the control and only the wall in front of me turned on, showing an exterior view of the city. The city was inside a tube-like structure suspended above the surface of Uranus, which extended several miles into the outer atmosphere. The diameter of the tube in which the cities were located was approximately fifty miles. There are many of these tube cities orbiting Uranus, some larger some smaller. Inside the city, there are no cars, buses, trucks, trains or aircraft. People get around in a complex system of trams that move vertically, horizontally and diagonally. The city is a wonderland of enchanted gardens and tropical forests that is populated by people and tame, exotic, animals. Some of the wildlife is similar to animals on Earth.

Because of the distance from the sun, there was little sunshine hitting the planet. However, the city was aglow with abundant sunlight, but the source of the artificial sunlight was unknown to me and unexplainable as well. Sunlight simply emanated out of the air and blanketed everything like real sunshine.

The suspended tube cities were not concentrated in one area of Uranus. Instead, the tubes were dispersed and separated by hundreds and thousands of miles. Located inside the outer walls of the tube cities were living quarters, work areas, learning centers and entertainment complexes.

There were no oceans as there are on Earth that I could see, but each city had many large lakes on platforms. Lakes, some with waterfalls, were nestled on humongous, floating platforms.

Bio-diversity exceeded that of Earth, at least tenfold. There were innumerable varieties of plants, insects and animal species of every conceivable type inside the cities. What was outside the living environments of the cities was not shown. The suspended tube cities were self-contained and able to move about the planet and off the planet like huge starships. Those city-ships absorbed energy and other essential resources from the host planet like cells inside a larger organism.

"Milton, can I apply for citizenship here? I think I like this place."

"No you can't. Your path is on a different course. For instance, most of the people with whom you traveled receive tours to some of the moons and get tourist views of the planet. But they remain unaware of the life forms that exist on Uranus. They also miss other phenomena only found off the beaten path, paths restricted to them. They don't get the 'exclusive' behind-the-scenes goodies that you are getting."

"Are the common people of Uranus aware of humans and entities like you, Milton?"

"The whole population is fully aware of other life in this solar system and the life that exists throughout the galaxy. Unlike on Earth, where most of the population remains in the dark about what is going on all around them, like babies in a nursery."

I was completely engrossed with what I saw on the screen concerning the city. There were tubes within tubes, all inhabited boroughs within the city structure. Some had unique styles and architectural designs, but I did not see unique cultures and diversity as we have on Earth. Cylinder or circular motifs dominate, whereas Earth structures are primarily rectangular. Everyone in the city appeared to be of the same race, excluding the non-indigenous life forms such as myself.

"There is something strangely familiar about this city, Milton. I have lived here in the past, is that right, Milton?

"You are correct, Michael. I was wondering if you would pick that up. You chose to go to Earth and be placed into a human body to experience yet another human existence, for reasons that will be divulged to you today."

7

MEMORIES FROM THE PAST

Like a broken dam in my head, memories burst into my mind from my past life on Uranus. I was a physicist and mathematician, among other things. I was not married, but had a lover. Marriage was not part of the culture in that city. There were no children and no old people. Everyone entered that city as spirits from other planets and were placed into fully formed and aware adult bodies. Age was not a factor. Everyone of that species or category was the same biological age, the equivalent of about thirty-five Earth years.

The bodies the people inhabited were nearly perfect biological machines built exclusively for pleasure. The bodies did not expire, become ill, or degrade in any way while they were in use. Bodies are created for the soul that inhabits them and destroyed when the soul moves up or away from that culture. Bodies are never reused, just like on Earth. The people consumed food for the pleasure of it and not for nutritional needs or survival requirements. Nutrients and energy are absorbed from a mineral rich atmosphere in the city that permeates around them like air.

In a previous body existence when I was a citizen of that city, I lived in a spacious and luxurious seven-room suite that was on the five-thousand-sixtieth floor, in one of the tube towers near the center of the city. Everyone lived in similar accommodations. Floor to ceiling height was more than twenty-five feet. Large balconies protruded out from each unit and overlooked spectacular views of the city.

Inclement weather was not a factor and never happened by chance inside of the cities. Rain was controlled and had a cleansing purpose for the city. There were no storms like those on Earth. The rain came down softly at predetermined intervals. Severe weather conditions did occur on the planet, but not inside of the cities and never affected the cities.

Biting insects, noise, and crime, were non-existent. Therefore, no need for doors or windows with screens and bars. Everything was open.

The city was a utopia and had no poverty, no wars, no hate, or transgressions between the inhabitants of any kind. Life was peaceful and joyful all the time.

Androids and other machines serviced the population, leaving the inhabitants to pursue occupations and leisure of their choosing.

Currency, credits, quotas, debits, allotments, and exchanges were unnecessary in that society. Everything needed or wanted was provided and available to all the inhabitants.

In that other life, I had several core friends and associates. But all citizens are friendly towards each other. The whole city was one large happy family. I had a primary lover, as did all of the inhabitants of the city. Our bodies were not anatomically similar to human bodies. There were however, male and female characteristics, without the reproductive organs. Genitalia were not as pronounced as that of humans, but infinitely more sensual.

All the inhabitants derived a certain pleasure from each other without physical contact, but physical contact was very intense and delightful. There were few monogamous relationships and abundant physical contact between the citizens. Public touching, embracing, and showing affection were the norm.

My primary lover was Neppti. Neppti was about to take a job on Earth and confronted me with that news.

"I'm considering taking the B786 assignment on Earth. What are your feelings about that?"

"That assignment is for sixty-three Earth years, am I correct?

"Yes it is."

"Why a new assignment so soon, Neppti?

"I owe Belii a favor. She goes by the name Linda on Earth, and her life took an unexpected turn and it might be more than she can handle. She has two children and a good husband, but is having problems with her main assignment. I think I can help her and bring B786 to fruition at the same time."

"Earth is a tricky place for you because you have been there more often than is advisable. I am surprised they are letting you take the assignment. Where do you go from there, Neppti?"

"They did try and talk me out of it, but I feel it's important to Belii. So, I'm going to risk it. I have two options after I complete my tour, both determined by my performance. I could return here or advance to another star system, depending on my actions and thoughts.

I embraced Neppti and our robes fell free to the floor. Touching bodies was extremely stimulating; kissing and embracing was mentally orgasmic. We embraced the equivalent of two Earth hours and rather than becoming exhausted afterwards, we emerged rejuvenated.

The act of embracing usually took place in a pool of warm liquid. The pool was located in the center of the main room of each apartment and was the equivalent of the family room. Since the inhabitants did not have families, the guest used the pools whenever they visited.

There was nothing taboo about the act of embracing, which was commonly done in public places wherever people congregated. The attraction-urge to have physical contact with others superseded all other desires. When it struck two people, they stopped what they were doing and stepped into any available pool in their vicinity. Pools of warm liquid were readily available everywhere in the city for that sole purpose.

Robes are the common clothing and are made of a lightweight fabric that never needs washing. In fact, they have no washing machines because everything is self-cleaning. Robes come in a variety of colors, but only two sizes, a male and female version. I had several in my closet, but I do not recall how they got there. Perhaps they came with the apartment.

Female robes were distinctly feminine and adorned with frills and lace, whereas the male version was plain.

Other than sandals and belts, there was no other clothing or accessories such as undergarments, sweaters, and coats. Robes had no purpose other than appearance. Nudity or hiding the body was not the reason for the wearing of clothing and neither was the temperature, which remained comfortable all the time.

The people in that city were similar to humans, but their bodies lacked functional genitalia and had no body hair. The female body was petite and cute, with small breasts. The male body was larger and trim. Obesity was genetically impossible. Yet, the people were not carbon copies of each other. Bodies and personalities were unique as they are with humans on Earth.

Neppti informed me that Belii was pregnant with a female child and would give birth in two Earth months. Neppti said that she was going to enter Belii's baby, to become her child a week after the birth. Belii would be abducted and her human fetus modified, or exchanged, with one suitable for Neppti's higher energy field.

I told Neppti that I preferred to wait more than a week before entering a newborn because the eyes are better developed and more focused by then. It has been awhile since I had been on Earth. Earth was at a higher level than it had been when I was there last. So perhaps it did not matter much when one entered the baby. Neppti agreed.

"You know there are many projects that need filling. Why don't you jump in and take one?" She asked me.

"There is one particular assignment that I had my eye on for some time, but I enjoyed being around you so much I couldn't make the jump. Now that you are going to Earth for a little time, I might do it. But this assignment has an ambiguous end date, so it could end in fifty Earth years or go longer. I have considered it because it has a good probability it will parallel yours. Best of all, there is a good chance it will lead to the same place you will go after the Earth assignment. Otherwise, I wouldn't take it."

Neppti reminded me that, "Earth has received a high number of returns from the First and Second World Wars, and is getting a huge influx of undesirables from two other star systems. These are not going to be easy assignments, as you know."

At that point, Milton blocked out the rest of my memories and snapped me back to the present.

"Milton, why did you interrupt my memories? I was enjoying immensely reminiscing about my past on this place."

"Your assignment is not complete, and it can easily be compromised at this stage, especially if I allow you more details about your former life here. I let you see a little because you have veered off track. We hope that some of the things you learned today will remedy that."

"Will I see Neppti again?"

"We'll discus that at a later date."

"It's amazing how much the human brain blocks out the past, and yet, the past remains integral in our memory. My mind nearly froze up from the sheer volume of memories and information that poured into my conscious mind from this place. There is so much more to existence, yet humans have no clue about any of it. How can people believe they originated from primordial pond scum on Earth? Why is that, Milton?"

"You know the answers to all those questions, but while you are locked into your human brain you are limited in what information you can process without external assistance from me."

"Can you give me a brief overview of what Earth is all about? I am a bit confused, since my knowledge base has been cutoff from me, as you so poignantly pointed out. It just seems that humans are getting a raw deal concerning knowledge and their place in this grand Milky Way galaxy."

"That kind of knowledge would interfere with the purpose of life on Earth. That's why people like you are limited in how much info you can access while on Earth. However, we are opening up some info to you so that you can drop hints for the few who are ready to accept a bigger view of life. Still, most people are not prepared, nor do they need this info, because not all humans on Earth have a purpose. Nor are humans on the same level of understanding. Instead, they are on many levels of "misunderstanding" and confusion. Many humans remain incarcerated on Earth as criminals. Their souls were sent to Earth from other planets and from other solar systems to serve time there. Some are repeats from Earth, criminals from previous lives on Earth that reincarnated back to prison Earth. Those people are not on Earth to learn anything, but are there only to serve hard or soft time, depending on their crimes. Planets like Earth are also places of learning through experiences, both good and bad experiences, which are designed to test a soul's worth, and to weed out the good from the bad, the weak from the strong.

Not all people on Earth are there for learning or punishment. Some souls are on vacation. Numerous entities, both human and nonhuman, go to Earth simply for the pleasure of it. The humans that are on vacation on Earth are there to enjoy themselves and encounter few problems during their lives. Their vacation was earned in former lives and situations. A few of the vacationers know who they are. The rest believe themselves extremely fortunate human beings."

ALIEN CONSPIRACIES

The interrogator walked back into the room. I sat up in my chair expecting the good news that I would be released and allowed to enjoy the rest of my stay in that fantastic city. I had a new appreciation for the people of Uranus, remembering I had been one of them gave me a good feeling. However, things didn't turn out quite as I expected.

"Mike, we have reason to believe that your being on Uranus has more to do with human interests than fluke ET joyrides. I'm sure you are aware that we have a human colony quarantined in our city, are you not?"

"I assumed that there are humans in your cities as guests or tourists. Are you suggesting there are other reasons they are here?"

"Very few are here as tourists because of the problems I mentioned earlier. Humans are carriers of bacteria and are not allowed inside our city. Humans have their own section that we provide for them. I'm not suggesting anything about why we have human colonies here. That info is confidential and none of your concern."

"How can a civilization as advanced as yours not have a handle on bacteria?"

"We do have a handle on it. We engineered it for the human digestive track and have isolated the germ on Earth and in a few other human colonies scattered around the solar system, including here on Uranus. Nevertheless, we have contingencies, but not for strays like you, who are migrating off Earth via supernatural means for purposes that even we do not quite understand. Therefore, we have implemented programs to deal with abductees who breach protocol and our security.

"So Einstein was wrong?——god does throw dice and everything is a crapshoot?"

"I don't know about god or dice, but there are many variables in this galaxy. You're being here, for instance, is one of them. It should not have happened and is un-welcomed."

"I was shown some memories of my past existence on Uranus. Am I not one of you?"

"That is information you shouldn't have been given. If what you say is true, a serious breach of compliance has occurred."

Interrogator left the room leaving me bewildered. I was back on square one concerning my dreadful situation.

"Milton, have you involved me in some intergalactic conspiracy?"

"Life in general is a conspiracy, Michael. There is a large human presence on Uranus, which unfortunately has complicated your particular situation. I'm working on it."

"Can't you simply abduct me off Uranus like you did when you took me from Earth?"

"The people of Uranus are highly advanced and can detect and capture my ship and detain me, if they find out that I am behind you being in their city. They can monitor your telepathic communications with me, but they can't tap into my mind. So don't repeat anything I say to you."

"Great! I get up and go for a simple walk in the park this morning and now I'm involved in extraterrestrial intrigue."

The door opened and an android entered the room. It did a scan on me with a beam emitted from its hand and stated that my bowels remained sealed. Therefore, I did not require a containment suit before he transported me from that room.

"Fantastic! I will put that information in my résumé."

The android said, "Follow me and don't try to run or escape. If you do, I will catch you and place you in a prison cell where you will remain for a long time."

"Does that mean I'm not free to go back to Earth?"

"I don't have answers for you. I have been instructed to take you to another location in the city."

The android took me over to an elevator and we entered. We were at one of the upper most levels of the city several miles up. The android took me down several floors beneath the city surface. The elevator rapidly descended many times the speed of free fall. I watched on a display that showed the floors we passed. Yet, I felt no sensation of movement. Merely a moment passed before the elevator reached its destination, and the android and I stepped out.

METROPOLIS BELOW TUBE CITY

The android walked away leaving me alone in the underground city. Human looking men walked by staring at me as if I was a freak or some strange anomaly. Then several of them came over, touched me, and poked me as if they were not sure what they were seeing. Then one of them spoke to me.

"You sure look human. Are you from Earth? Do you speak English?"

"I'm from Earth, and obviously I speak English," I replied.

"You came out of that elevator. Humans are prohibited in that city. You were in that city, so who are you? How did you get in that city if you are human?"

Everyone in the crowd looked at me intently, waiting for my answer. I was not sure how to answer since I did not know what I could reveal to total strangers. I was in some god-forsaken place that was located in the bowels of a giant gas planet over a billion miles from

Earth and some strange humans were asking me questions. It couldn't get any crazier than that!

I decided to avoid answering his questions. Instead, I asked my own questions.

"First, tell me what humans are doing on Uranus when most of the human world on Earth hardly believes we have been to Earth's moon?"

They all looked at each other not sure what they could confide to me since they did not know who or what I was. Then another man standing behind the crowd spoke up.

"Bet you are hungry?"

"They gave me some wafers in the city above and told me that humans are not allowed to eat normal food because of the bacteria in our system. I'm not hungry, but are you saying that you can eat normal human type food down here?"

"In this area you can eat anything you want. I never heard about bacteria being a problem before. Have any of you guys?"

Everyone shook their heads implying they were not aware of such a rule, while keeping their gaze firmly on me the whole time. The man who asked me if I were hungry introduced himself as Joe. He asked that the others go about their business while he questioned me in private. The crowd dispersed with their curiosity still peaked and some talked among themselves as they walked away while looking back at Joe and me.

Joe said, "Let's go where we can talk without drawing a crowd. There is a pub down a ways from here. Follow me."

The area we were in looked like a rundown shopping and entertainment district where basic supply shops and some adult diversions dominated the few storefronts. Joe and I walked the equivalent of two blocks and entered a pub. It was a typical redneck-looking bar with a sparse selection of liquor bottles on glass shelves behind a synthetic-looking mahogany bar.

The place had a raw turn-of-the-century cowboy look and feel to it. The bar did not resemble a modern drinking or eating establishment. There was an antique jukebox, stools around the bar, a few tables and booths, and a broken down pool table with boxes stacked on it. The place was empty of patrons, but the old jukebox was playing Sinatra tunes! Somehow, that seemed stranger than being a billion miles from Earth.

Joe and I sat at one of the tables and an android came from a backroom and handed us menus. I took one out of curiosity and looked through it while Joe ordered a beer. I did not ask for anything because my system was sealed and I did not know how food and drink would affect me. Besides, I was not too sure about Joe, who resembled a character from a James Cagney gangster movie. For all I knew, this place was a prison colony under the city that I was dumped into because the powers weren't sure what else to do with me. I attempted to keep the mood light to cover my apprehension of Joe and the other men, who follow us to the bar but remained outside. The menu items surprised me and I blurted out, "Hamburgers and Fish! Don't tell me you guys have cows and oceans up here?"

"Some of our food comes from Earth and other places in the solar system. Our food gets special processing and packaging and we receive shipments twice a week."

"What the hell are humans doing on Uranus anyway? And how is it possible to travel that distance from Earth?"

"Since you have to ask me those kinds of questions, I can't give you the answers. The important questions for me: Who are you? How and why are you here, Mike?"

"A space alien brought me to Uranus and somehow I fell through the bureaucratic cracks."

"Heck, that is how some of us got here, too. We call it the ET express. But that falling through the cracks does not quite jive. Those entities upstairs do not let humans 'fall through the cracks.' There is certainly something else going on, but let's not split hairs about it right now. There are several thousand humans on this planet, but I cannot give you an exact number because no one knows how many. There are covert operations within covert operations. Then to complicate matters further, there is you. We have been told that no human can enter the city that you were in. Yet, you came out of that elevator. There isn't a man or women here that wouldn't give their right arm to see what you have seen inside that city. So, what can you tell me about that city above us?"

"It's your basic utopia. The inhabitants live exquisite, uncomplicated lives, unlike humans on Earth where we can't seem to get into the groove of what life is really about. The city is void of all the problems that plague humanity on Earth and I suppose here, too.

These people seem to know all the answers that have eluded humans on Earth, or most of them anyway. Much of Earth's technology comes from them, if you can believe that."

"I can believe that! All our equipment, the androids, and the cities that we humans inhabit were made and provided to us by the inhabitants of the city above us. Still, we do not get to interact directly with them. We communicate through the androids, but the androids do not tell us anything about their masters. However, we are participating in the construction of a satellite city orbiting Uranus. It is primarily a learning experience for us. Everything here is a learning experience."

"How did you get picked for this assignment, Joe? Did you volunteer to be here? People from Earth don't just up and disappear if they have family and friends, do they? Or were you born here?"

"I was not born here, although, some of those you met earlier are from here and other places and planets besides Earth. Anyway, thousands of people disappear from cities around the world on Earth every year without a trace. They gave those statistics to me when they approached me for this assignment many years ago. I was an officer in Special Forces and was stationed in Vietnam when my commanding officer made me the offer to come here. My grandparents, who passed away shortly after I joined the army, raised me. As far as I know, I am an only child. I never knew my father or my mother and I had no wife or children. My commanding officer asked me if I wanted to relocate to another planet in this solar system. It took me awhile to realize he was not kidding and I accepted the offer. Once I did, they took me during a firefight my platoon got into during a routine patrol. After that battle, I was listed as missing in action and the next thing I knew, I was on a spaceship to Uranus. Talk about mind-blowing. I have been back to Earth several times under a new identity. I received my PhD in sociology at an ivy league university where I was enrolled as a foreign exchange student."

I was sitting with my back to the front door listening to Joe, distracted by his riveting story. Then one of the men who stopped me earlier when I first got off the elevator walked into the pub. The man looked at Joe to acknowledge that he could come over to our table. I glanced back behind me and saw him, but I did not think much of it, believing he was going to join us for a drink.

I turned back to face Joe when the man walked up behind me and hit me over the head with a blackjack. I dropped to the floor as if shot in the head. The two men then carried my limp body into a freight elevator at the back of the pub. (I know the details because Milton filled me in later)

Milton told me that the elevator went down several floors and stopped. Joe and the other guy pulled my body out of the elevator, dragged me a few yards, and left me slumped on the floor. They then returned to the elevator and went back up. A few minutes passed before I regained consciousness. I awoke with a massive headache and some blood on the back of my shirt and neck. I felt the back of my head and realized that I been shanghaied and probably left to die. At first, I thought perhaps they had shot me in the head and I nearly went into shock thinking about that scenario. But the bleeding had stopped and there didn't appear to be a hole in my skull that I could feel. But there was a painful lump.

I looked around, still in a daze and not sure where I was. It didn't take long for me to remember that I was not on Earth, but in a very strange place. As I regained my thoughts, I questioned if there was anyone in the solar system I could trust.

I gather the strength to stand up and I staggered a bit before straightening completely. I was in a large cavernous place that looked like a warehouse filled with odd-looking containers. The equipment, or machinery, seemed to go on forever. The place was lit up with artificial daylight, the same stuff that was in the city above. The area appeared deserted. There were no sounds or signs of mechanical or biological entities. I was alone, and I felt alone to my core. That was an awful feeling.

Rows upon rows of presumably large machinery encased in smooth metallic coverings were everywhere. Whatever they were, machinery or something else, they did not make any sound and did not vibrate like Earth machinery. A painful silence hung in the air and it seemed like I was the only man alive in the universe. I felt abandoned and sank into a severe depression.

I looked at my watch and it was only 7PM Earth time. I could not believe it was the same day. That nutty odyssey I was trapped in was moving very slowly. I was not convinced that my watch was working because it seemed like I had been away from Earth at least two or three days, if not longer.

"Milton, can you hear me? I am tired of all this fun and games. What is the motive behind the cloak and dagger secrecy crap? I don't care that humans are on this stinking planet! I don't care that intelligent life other than humans exist. Give me back my normal, fucking life!"

Milton did not respond. I speculated that perhaps the place, the room, that I was in, blocked out Milton's telepathy. That was unnerving since he was my only link back to Earth.

I went to the elevator from where I presumed they dumped me out of. I wanted to take it back up, but there were no buttons. The elevators operated through some means unknown to me.

The stress wore me down. I was now hungry, thirsty and pissed off so badly that I could not think straight. Being clueless about what was going on and helpless to do anything about it irked the heck out of me.

The icing on the cake was the fact that the bozos had the nerve to plug up my gut without giving me instructions about what to do in the strange situation I now found myself. I did not even know if I could eat a rat without doing internal damage to my body organs. I did need to pee and since there were no bathrooms, I took a leak on the elevator door.

"What a crazy day this turned out to be!" I shouted out in a desperate voice while standing in front of the elevator and pounding on the door. Realizing the futility of yelling at the elevator door, I turned around and headed into the cavern in search of another way out. The cavern seemed to go on forever. There were large tubes and pipes running along the tall ceilings, but not connected to the large machinery below. The machines, or whatever they were, looked menacing in their silent and monolithic eeriness. I walked around them trying to figure out what they might be. They had no markings and did not give up their secrets. As time dragged on and I had little luck finding a way out of that cavern, my mind conjured up frightful images of large alien cocoons, rather than machinery, I was freaking myself out. I walked for forty minutes in one direction and saw no sign of man, android, or rat. Hunger does crazy things to the mind and if a rat happened by, I would have attempted to catch it and eat it. I hate to think what I would do if I had to go longer than a day without real food. The scenery for as far as I could see was carbon copies of noiseless, cocooned, contraptions and endless runs of ductwork above them. Presumably, those cocoons served the upper world in some way.

The floor of the cavern was a solid, smooth material similar to concrete, but black like asphalt. The walls and ceiling were gray and made from the same concrete-looking material. Floor to ceiling height was about fifty feet. The cavern was not like a straight and narrow hallway. It was more like a huge underground mine, with thick columns spaced evenly apart every 300 feet.

After about on hour of aimless wondering, I spotted something in the distance of the cavern that was moving towards me. It was some sort of vehicle and it was traveling fast. The machine looked like it was going to hit me, so I moved from what I believed was its path. I did so, the vehicle intelligently corrected itself to my new position. I could not outrun the thing and it seemed I was not going to be able to dodge it either. I turned away from it and braced for impact, expecting to become road-kill. Amazingly, the vehicle zoomed right up to me and nearly touched me, but to my relief it stopped dead cold. Mysteriously, the android driving it did not fly off, as one might expect from such a sudden stop. My conservative estimate was that the vehicle was moving in excess of 150 miles an hour. Kinetic energy and inertia did not seem to exist at those realms of technology.

"What manner of physics do these people operate?" I asked myself.

The vehicle was a tandem two-seater hovercraft without a top and looked like a torpedo.

The Android told me to get in.

I jumped in the backseat and the vehicle took off like a shot, in reverse. Rather than make a u-turn, the vehicle headed back in the direction from which it had come and rapidly picked up speed. The android was facing the front when the craft approached, but was now facing the rear. The android's seat swiveled and now he was facing forward. My seat swiveled at the same time his did and I was looking straight ahead. No windshield in the back or in the front, yet there was no wind blowing against my face as we traveled at a high rate of speed. The miles of cocooned machinery, like telephone poles on a highway, became a blur due to the speed we were going.

The strange vehicle had no steering mechanism or other visible controls. It operated solely by the android's computer brain, or so it seemed. I did not ask the android any questions knowing from past experiences that androids never gave out useful information.

After traveling some distance, the vehicle approached what appeared to be a solid wall. The android did not slow down and continued towards the wall at breakneck speed. I shut my eyes and braced for impact. At the very last moment, an opening appeared in the wall and the vehicle shot through it like a bullet. Then the opening shut instantly behind us. The opening and closing was like the shutter on a camera, faster than a blink of an eye. I was deep into the rabbit hole.

Should we manage to stick our head through the curtain of existence, initially we will not comprehend anything, and then awe

8

HUMAN TOWN

We entered a bustling, futuristic city inhabited by humans (according to my android guide). The vehicle continued into the city streets filled with similar vehicles, also operated by androids. No stoplights or signs at the city intersections, but vehicles streamed through cross traffic without slowing or stopping in perfect synchronization. It took awhile before I stopped flinching at every intersection that we entered.

The city with its tall buildings was subterranean in the sense that it was under the tube city. The city above was visible from the atrium ceiling above human town as if the town (human town) was inside a huge aquarium. Artificial light shined as bright as the sun inside of human town. The artificial light rays hitting my skin felt like they were coming from our sun. It was a beautiful sunny day below several miles of clouds on a planet that barely received any real sunlight.

The metropolis was huge and completely different in appearance from the cities above it. The city had a human feel and look to it, except for the androids and the strange vehicular driving systems. Much of the architecture and street layout was identical to cities on Earth, but things operated very differently here.

The android gave me a tour of the town without my having asked for it. There were high-rise apartments, office complexes and even a suburb on the outskirts of the city. They had the usual ingredients of every metropolis: schools, hospitals, parks and a prison. The prison was not surprising since a couple of thugs had assaulted me earlier. I was not sure if those thugs belonged to that city or were part of a human covert operation that was taking place on Uranus.

The android read my mind that I was hungry and offered me some crackers.

"I'm not authorized to give you human food and drink, but I can give you some wafers and a special liquid to drink. Would you like these items?"

"Yes, I would, thank you. By the way, are you taking me somewhere in particular in this city or only killing time before you kill me?"

"I am killing time until I receive further instructions. Is there somewhere you wish to go and see while here or something you would like to do?"

"I would like to go for a walk it that park we passed when we first came into this city, if I could."

I had walked over an hour before the android picked me up, but I was accustomed to walking on hour or two every other day. It was how I relaxed. I needed to relax in a park setting after my ordeal and I also suspected things could get weirder before they got better. The android took me directly to the forest. The vehicle was capable of flying without the use of wings. The android parked the vehicle in the parking lot of the nature trail and let me off.

"I will remain here and come and get you when I am notified to bring you in," the android said.

"No hurry," I told him.

There were women and men with baby strollers and people riding bicycles, walking and jogging just like at the park in my neighborhood that morning. For an instant, I felt like I was back on Earth. However, the parking lot was full of strange looking vehicles, chauffeured by robots. That was a stark reminder I was not in Kansas anymore.

That park had trees nearly as tall as the Sequoia in California. It also had many species of insects that I had never seen before. The climate was tropical and many varieties of vegetation with colorful blooms and tantalizing fragrances bordered both sides of the walking trail. Strange looking insects glowed under the shade of the forest canopy. Some crawled around the decaying tree trunks covered in moss and looking like critters with headlights. Large fluorescent winged butterflies gave the forest a feel of enchantment and helped me erase some of the stress that had built up.

After about twenty minutes, the android pulled up next to me on a two-seater bicycle and told me to jump on. I took a liking to that android, even though it was only a machine without emotions and no real concern for me. We rode back to the parking lot where the android parked the bike in the bicycle corral and we jumped into the flying vehicle and left the park.

The android took me to an office building near the center of the city and dropped me off at the entrance. It handed me a piece of paper with a room number on it and told me to report there. I entered the building, took the elevator up to the fifth floor and found the office with the number that was on the note. I entered into a reception area and walked to the reception window. There was no one behind the window and no one sitting in the waiting room. I took a seat and waited. Unfortunately, there were no magazines to read. I would have enjoyed seeing something about their culture and strange way of life. I tried contacting Milton while I sat there twiddling my thumbs in nervous anticipation.

"Milton, if you can hear me, let me know. I have a wife at home and she is going to wonder where the hell I am. Can I get a message to her, please?"

No answer.

After about ten minutes, a woman in a laboratory gown entered the reception room and asked me to come with her. She looked familiar, but I could not place where I had seen her before. I followed her into a hallway and we walked past several rooms with medical-looking equipment, but no doctors or patients. It seemed that she and I were the only ones in that place.

"You look familiar. Do I know you from somewhere?" I asked her.

"Yes, we have met before."

She then led me into a room that looked like a hospital operating room. The sight and smell of the room put a knot in my stomach and it made me uneasy. She noticed my discomfort and hesitation to enter the room and tried to calm me.

"Relax, Mike, this is routine and you have done it a number of times before."

"I have no idea what you are talking about. If I have done this many times, my memory has been blocked, so feel free to refresh it for me!"

"You are involved with an invisible society as you probably know by now. A secret society and it must remain that way. We have had a few glitches this time and you are still alive only because you have one heck of a powerful team working on your behalf. Those men meant to kill you. Instead, you only ended up with a bump on your head. Someone put a block on the communications implant you have in your body and for a brief time we lost contact with you."

"So how did you find me?"

"We activated a backup implant. But because they can monitor implant signals, we waited until the last minute and then made our move to rescue you."

"So games continue to be played even at these higher levels?"

"This is not as simple as a game. This is the real deal and things can get complicated very fast. Problems happen every now and then. Human bodies, which are nothing more than complex machines, have antibodies to fight off germs and other intruders. Physical entities, regardless of how complex and advanced, remain subject to viruses. For instance, software used by silicon-based electronic computers is susceptible to viruses and a host of other maladies that are caused or created by humans and higher up entities."

"Is that why Milton isn't in constant communication with me?"

"Partly. He is continuously changing his telepathic frequencies to remain incognito. Now remove all your clothing, Michael, and lay down on the table on your back, please."

I removed my clothes and got on the table. Two androids came into the room and to the table I was laying on. One of the androids clamped my arms to the table and the other clamped my legs. They did it so quickly that I had no time to react.

"Is this necessary? You are freaking me out, you know!"

"I told you to relax, Michael, and look on the screen that is located on the wall to your right."

The screen displayed an X-ray of my abdomen in a perfect three-dimensional and nauseatingly real view of my innards. Thank god for skin to hide all those not so splendid details inside of us! There were three "alien" objects inside my intestinal track.

"What the hell are those things doing inside of my gut? Jesus Christ, people, are you telling me that I'm nothing more than a courier for alien contraband?"

"Your body synthesizes certain enzymes and is a unique machine that you possess, Michael. That's partly the reason why you are in this program of ours."

The android that clamped down my legs directed a probe that came out from the bottom of the surgical table and inserted it into my rectum. I squirmed and tried to pull lose from the table, but could not budge. I yelled obscenities at the android and before I knew it, the procedure was over. But my anger ratcheted up quickly and I was fuming.

"Look at the screen, Michael. The items are now gone. That didn't hurt much, did it?"

I could not answer immediately without shouting more obscenities and gave myself a little time to calm down before I responded to her.

"No, it didn't hurt, but the whole idea is repulsive—thank you!"

"All in a day's work, Michael. Besides, I did not think it was repulsive. After all, the human body is only a machine, not much different than the androids that clamped you down. Emotions and desires are programs installed into the human brain, similar to software that we upload into computers. Moreover, your soul is a sort of software that is loaded into the human mind and placed at the controls inside the human brain. The soul is similar to a pilot in the cockpit of an airplane or you in the driver's seat of your car. Souls simply push buttons inside physiological machines (human bodies) and animate them. Your soul, you, is inside the control room, which is your brain. The soul controls, or is controlled by, the other software humans call emotions. But you are not your brain or your body, nor your emotions, which are only software.

"Are you finished playing with my machine? Or is there more? Do I get cargo for the return trip, too?"

"No cargo from me, but that's not to say you are returning to Earth empty. They will probably block that memory if they do insert items in your abdomen or elsewhere in your body. I am not blocking this memory because Milton told me to leave it intact so that you can access it later when you get back to Earth. While I have you on the table, I would like to extract semen from you—the natural way. Have any objections, Michael?"

Not waiting for my answer, she slipped out of her garment revealing a gorgeous body! My attitude quickly changed and I was instantly under her seductive spell. The androids removed my shackles and I remained on the table with my arm propped under my head.

"God, you are beautiful!" I told her.

I reached up, took her arm, and pulled her onto the table with me as the table automatically lowered to the floor. We rolled off the table and onto a soft warm floor, embraced in passionate ecstasy. Moments after copulation, we remained embraced.

"Are you presently seeing anyone?" I asked her. "I mean, are you married or have anyone special in your life?"

"I'm not that kind of girl, Michael. I am not the dating or marrying type. I have a modified human body, but I am not human, nor am I available, but thanks for asking! I'm really not much different than you, Michael, but I think you know that. How much you know, I'm not certain."

"I was allowed to remember a brief period of my life in the tube city upstairs from this town. From there, I remember going to planet Earth and being inserted into the body I am in now. That was two weeks after it was born. Milton is bringing me up to speed about other things. And now here I am with you gathering even more interesting and definitely more stimulating information!"

"Your semen from this encounter will produce triplets inside of me, two males and one female. I will not carry the babies to term, however. The embryos will then be removed from my body and inserted into three other women living in this city. The women will carry the babies to term and give birth to them as their own children, never knowing that a switch took place. You and I have the fun and easy part, don't you agree, Michael?"

"So, I have a modified human body as you do and our bodies propagate behind the scenes without the knowledge of 'real' humans? Will humans ever know about this hidden world we exist in?"

"There are some humans that suspect something is amiss because of abduction stories and claims of missing fetuses and the taking of sperm and ova. But the general population will remain in the dark about what is really happening."

She got up and helped me up. While holding my hand, she led me to a room with a circular and spacious shower stall. She took me into the shower stall and washed me down. I returned the favor. The warm water in the shower made it seem like heaven and we embraced again and began making intense love once more. It was as if we were standing under a waterfall from a warm mountain stream with the multiple showerheads spraying sensuous waves of scented liquid onto our bodies.

(Between kissing) "Do I have to go back to Earth? Please tell me no."

"This is a freebie, Michael, and it is frowned upon by the higher ups, so don't tell Milton that we splurged a little while in the shower. But yes, you have to go back to Earth. However, not until I'm through with you!"

"Please god, don't let her ever be through with me!"

That comment made her laugh and she pinched my nose and even playfully shook it.

The water in the shower stopped, the shower stall glowed brightly for a few seconds and we were instantly dry. We walked out of the shower while she continued holding my hand and led me into an adjacent room. The room looked like a kitchen. It had the usual kitchen stuff—a refrigerator, sink, and a cook top built into a futuristic-looking countertop. She took me to a chair that was against one of the walls in the kitchen and sat me down. We remained naked and she went to the refrigerator about fifteen feet away on the opposite wall from where I was sitting and pulled out a bottle of strange-looking liquid. She poured some into a glass and brought it over to me.

"What is it?" I asked her in a curious, but somewhat suspicions voice.

"Nectar reserved for the gods. Try it, you will love it!"

"I'm a god?"

"You were in the shower, Michael," she giggled.

I took a sip of the nectar and jumped up from my chair unable to restrain my delight with the magical liquid.

"WOW....!" I shouted.

I took another mouth full of the precious concoction.

"This isn't going to hurt me, is it? How much of it can I drink?"

"You can drink as much as you want, Michael. The fridge is filled with it."

(Between gulps) "How come you are not drinking any of this fabulous stuff?"

"I'm on the clock."

"Do you usually walk around naked while on the job?"

"Only when I want to keep someone aroused. Are you aroused, Michael?"

There was no hiding just how much I was aroused and smiled back at her without saying a word.

While sitting comfortably on my chair eagerly awaiting her next move, she walked over to me holding something in her clasped hand. She stopped inches in front of me, her breast nearly touching my face.

"Do you want to suckle from them, Michael?"

I set my drink on the counter next to me and was all over them as if they were manna from heaven. I was at the boiling point of ecstasy and then she pulled away from me and placed the objects she was holding seductively into my mouth—one at a time, with her fingers, and then closed my lips with a kiss.

"Swallow them, Michael."

I did as she requested. I was intoxicated with sexual bliss and the love potion she gave me to drink. She clasped her hands on my face, gave me another passionate kiss and then pulled away, handing back my drink.

"Drink all of it, Michael."

I upended the cup, drank it all and handed the empty cup back to her. Before I could ask for more, I melted into her arms and was out cold.

Everyday brings something new to the table for those who care to take notice.

9

ONE OF THE MOONS
AROUND URANUS

I regained consciousness and found myself lying on a bed inside a glass dome. The dome was part of a small alien outpost that consisted of more than a dozen glass-domed structures that were interspersed within a ten-acre sector (somehow, I knew those details). The domes were different sizes that ranged from twenty feet in diameter for the smallest one, to more than sixty feet for the larger ones. The domes did not connect to each other via surface covered walkways that I could see. Whether underground tunnels connected them, I had no way of knowing. I was alone in one of the smaller domes. The domes were made of a glass-like substance and I had a panoramic view of Uranus and its rings and could see some of the other moons.

I found it difficult to restrain my excitement about the spectacle before me and loudly proclaimed, "My GOD! It keeps getting better and better!" That was the best view of the planet I had to that point.

I retained most of my memories about the encounter with the female lab technician. Or perhaps she was a doctor, she never said. I was not sure who she was or how she fit into the mystery that was unfolding around me, but she left me tantalized. She must have repaired my bruised head because it did not hurt anymore. I presumed that the encounter with her took place only moments earlier, but had no memory of leaving the building or the city, or traveling to that moon. I looked at my watch; about an hour had passed since the time I remembered looking at it a few minutes before I entered her office. I felt great. No aftereffects from the alien wine, and I had four or more glasses of that stuff.

The bed I was laying on was extremely comfortable and was reclined to give me a perfect view of the lunar landscape and the other mysterious objects floating in the moon sky. I had nothing to do but savor the spectacular view and to contemplate what some of those other alien ships or satellites were doing buzzing around in the sky above me. There were several objects in orbit around the moons and the planet. Some of the UFOs pulsated with colorful rays like beacons or a type of Morse code communication method. Milton did not explain them because he said they did not apply to what I needed to know.

After relaxing a few minutes in the dome, I saw Milton's ship materialized above the dome as if it had come out of a time warp or parallel dimension. It hovered above the dome for a minute and then moved near and made contact with the dome. Once the edge of the craft touched the dome, a seal formed and an opening into the dome manifested. I remained on the bed intently watching this strange miracle unfold. Milton poked his head through the opening, gave me a wink, then jumped out of the hole and slowly landed next to where I was resting. He was in his freaky alien costume.

"Milton, why would I want to go back to my life on Earth after what I have seen and experienced today?"

"I can erase all of it from your memory if you like, Michael."

"NO! If I can keep the memories, I want them."

"Good, because we want you to keep these memories. They are part of your assignment on Earth from this point on. I will go into it in more detail later."

"Milton, what are humans doing on Uranus?"

"Same as they are doing on Earth and other planets and moons in this solar system. They are learning to find and define their place in the galaxy. A few will do it in the course of a few lifetimes. For others it will take several lifetimes. But some will not make it and they will be put into storage for special treatment. There will be a few that are deactivated permanently."

"Put into storage? Are you talking about souls?"

"Your soul is anchored to your body, strapped in tightly via your blood. Without a physical living body anchoring the soul, the soul is free to go wherever it chooses or drifts. The body is a prison that is escape proof until death, but there are loopholes. Furthermore, no one dies until their time is up or they are 'allowed' to die. Suicides are returned immediately to another baby body somewhere in this solar system and they start over again, unless there is an acceptable reason for the suicide."

"So how do I fit in to all this? Am I a prisoner on Earth?"

"You, Michael, are on assignment from Uranus and we let you remember only a sliver of that reality. You will return to Uranus once your job on Earth is completed and your body dies on Earth. But that could change, depending on circumstance during this assignment. Either way, after a short time on Earth, or back on Uranus, should you end up back on Uranus, you will leave this solar system altogether, and go to a double star system deep in the interior of this galaxy."

"How is it possible to travel the kinds of distances that are involved in crossing the galaxy?"

"It isn't possible while in a human body."

"So I have to die before I leave the solar system?"

"No, you only have to leave your body behind until you return."

Without warning me, Milton then exited his body and his outer shell fell to the floor like a thick rubber suit. Milton was now a brilliant orb of energy about the size of a baseball and was floating next to the bed that I was laying on. Startled, I jumped off the other side of the bed and stood there looking at Milton as if I were looking at an apparition.

"How much of this can my mind take in one day, Milton? You keep pulling mind-blowing tricks out of your hat, and now this!"

"If you were the average, normal human, your mind would have failed long before this point and we would have simply erased these things from your memory and returned you back to your bed at home.

Nevertheless, I unlock things in your mind in a careful manner on this labyrinth-like journey to avoid a mental systems crash. I meander in my technique because of the fragile human brain that you are presently occupying. You did come from an advanced stage of existence with a purpose and a mission, and you should be able to handle these strange things, as I slowly and carefully peel away deeply embedded illusions that most humans are encased in shortly after birth. Your mission would have been compromised had you known who you were. If you knew, then others would know, and they would have interfered with our work. And our work is never done."

"Now, that I know a lot more than I did yesterday, what is to stop 'them'—whoever they are—from stopping you and me from completing this mission? I still have no clue what we are doing."

"You are nearing the end of your mission and we will have to take our chances with the little info we have given you today. Obviously, we cannot give you all the details and we will continue to be ambiguous with some of what we do give you, to keep a step ahead of 'them.' The only way I can describe 'them' is a two-party political system like the one you have in America. Both parties want the same thing for the American people, but they disagree on the methods to achieve their goals. It's actually much more complicated than that, but until you are higher up the ladder, you will not understand."

"I'm standing here talking to a floating, glowing, ball of light! What more is there to understand? Not that I understand this crazy phenomena, or much of the crazy stuff I have been part of today."

"Oh believe me, Michael, it gets better still. Are you ready to take off your ball and chain and become a glowing ball of light also?"

"Is that a euphemism for killing me, Milton?"

"Dying is the only other way to get out of that body you are in. But I have the authority - the key - to open your brain and release you from the tethers that are holding you inside your body without killing you. Are you game?"

"That whole idea is freaking me out. Can I have some of that wine that woman gave me back on Uranus before you do your thing on me? The wine made everything feel so good. I had no cares, no fear, as I do now."

"You won't feel a thing, Michael."

Milton's bright orb zoomed next to me and touched my head with his glowing essence and my body dropped to the floor like a sack of potatoes. Two glowing orbs were floating in the dome next to each other.

"My mind feels the same, Milton, but I feel much lighter as if a large weight were removed from me, physically speaking. I presume that crumpled body on the floor is me? It does not look anything as I thought it would look. Should you put my body on the bed or something? It looks uncomfortable in its crumpled state and I assume I have to return to that awful looking thing, don't I?"

"Yes, you will be put back into that 'thing,' so give me a hand and we will place your ball and chain on the bed. Grab hold of the arms and I will get the legs."

"Grab with what? I'm a freaking fuzzy ball of light for crying out loud!"

Milton flew towards my crumpled body on the floor and grabbed the legs. I floated around the room gently bouncing off the glass dome then back to the floor and back up again towards the apex of the dome. I did not know how to stop myself. I was a ping-pong ball in slow motion bouncing between floor and ceiling. "Will wonders ever cease, Milton?"

"Sure they will cease when you get through monkeying around and give me a hand with your body, Michael."

"How do I control my direction, Milton?"

"Oh, that's right. You have never done this before. Focus on where you want to be and you are there."

I slowly drifted near my body down on the floor, hit the floor and bounced back toward the dome again. Meanwhile, Milton picked up my body by coming into contact with the legs, and as if Milton was an electromagnet, he attached to my legs and lifted my body off the floor. My limp body dangled from a ball of light—Milton. Milton then positioned the head at one end of the bed and slowly maneuvered the rest of my body onto the bed. The moon we were on had very little gravity, but the artificial gravity inside the dome was similar to that on Uranus. The gravity was slightly less than Earth gravity, but it was enough to provide a sense of normality to humans like me. Milton's orb of energy managed to lift my 190 pounds of pure muscle off the floor and onto the bed, as if it were a ragdoll.

I watched that take place while simultaneously admiring the planet Uranus, which was fascinating. I was aware of two mind-blowing events at once. I was not sure which of the two scenes were more intriguing. After a bit of bouncing from floor to ceiling, I suddenly became stationary up against the glass dome at its highest point. I was not sure if I had caused myself to stop or if I came to rest by some other power that I was not yet aware existed.

"Cool! I can see in panorama! What is keeping me from going through the glass, Milton? The glass feels like a solid surface, but I thought we were like ghosts or spirits. Shouldn't we simply pass through solid things?"

"You can't see yourself, but you are the size of a golf ball. The level of awareness determines our energy aura. You are twice that of the average person on Earth, but considerably less than where you need to be to attain real autonomy. You will achieve it in your next stage. Not Uranus, but the place you will go to once you return to Uranus after your Earth assignment. By the way, all muscle?"

"You have no sense of humor for someone with such a large aura, Milton. So Freud was right, size does matter?"

"We are not talking size of ego or libido. Have you given any consideration to being a comedian, Michael? You are good at it, you know. Yes, size makes all the difference when it comes to knowledge and awareness. You can penetrate the glass barrier by willing yourself through it, but then what would you do? You will drift into space and space is very big for those without a destination. You might be able to find your way back to places you once inhabited like Earth and Uranus, but then what would you do? Haunt your old hangouts with other lost spirits?"

"Are you implying that ghosts are people without guides—souls lost in space?"

"They are entities who have lost their way. They are without purpose. Souls searching for what no longer exists, and never will for them, because they failed to put forth the effort to create something meaningful while they were alive on Earth. Most souls in that category will not linger long on Earth or in their next station. Those souls will be sent back to reincarnate on one of the many Earth-like planets in the galaxy. Some of them receive opportunities to excel or squander; others will simply serve time. There is more to it and you will learn more later, but not today. Suffice it to say, that you need a guide like me now that you are out of your body or else you will simply drift away. Without a destination, we drift helplessly on the waves of space, whether we are in a physical form or a 'freaking ball of fuzzy energy,' as you put it. I'm going to take you across the galaxy to a star system many thousands of light years away, so stay near me if you don't want to get lost in space."

"Don't mess with my fuzzy ball mind, Milton, seriously! You would not leave me behind if you and I become separated somehow, would you? You did lose track of me while I was on Uranus, remember?"

"I never lost track of you, Michael. That was a ploy to throw others off your trail. Besides, you are not free to go anywhere on your own while out of your body. You remain under my charge and responsibility. You could not get away from me even if you tried. You can only drift away from me perhaps a hundred yards in any direction before hitting an invisible barrier. In essence, you are tethered to me for your own protection. Follow me, Michael."

I followed Milton and squinted as if I had eyes that could squint as I passed through the glass of the dome. I anticipated that the solid barrier would snare me somehow or that I would bounce off it as I had done several times already. Instead, I slipped through it with the ease of light going through glass.

Milton and I flew around Uranus and then into its atmosphere and then out again like a pair of pixies. We then traveled through the rings of Uranus and circled around a few of the moons going low to the surface on some of them, strictly for the spectacular in-my-face view.

"This is too much! I feel like a god, like superman. Thank you, Milton!"

"Don't thank me, Michael. I just work here."

"So, we are going to travel great distances without a ship?"

"Ships slow you down. Nothing travels faster than the free spirit does. However, there are many kinds of ships. Some travel through galaxies by making dimensional leaps through space-time. Some use magnetic waves and a number of other exotic and supernatural means for transporting physical matter from one place to another. The movement of 'matter' requires energy. Moving matter is not necessary in many situations. Matter is everywhere and it can be manipulated by us on location for most purposes."

TWO ORBS ABOVE MARS

"Whoa, how did we get here so fast? So you blink and we are there, or here or wherever?"

"We can fly like Superman, Michael, and travel slowly through the solar system taking the scenic route, which I recommend when you have more time. We are on a schedule today, so I am blinking our way across the solar system to demonstrate a few possibilities and realities that exist throughout the galaxy. I thought that I would give you a sneak peek of the planets in your neck of the woods along the way."

During our brief stop, I managed to notice other orbs and UFOs coming and going from the planet Mars. It looked like a busy place and I asked Milton about what was going on with Mars. He told me he might tell me later.

"Are there any other planets you would like to see before we shoot out towards the center of the Milky Way galaxy, Michael?"

"Take me to the stars, Milton."

In an instant, Milton and I are 99.5 percent to our destination. We stopped several light-years from a star cluster and were many thousands of light-years away from Earth.

"My physics teacher is never going to believe this is possible, Milton!"

"Good, don't tell him."

We were deep into the darkness of space, except that it was not dark towards the center of the galaxy where huge clusters of stars lit up large parcels of space with brilliant, colorful luminosity. Dark nights out there were completely impossible. Each of the hundreds of clusters contained thousands of star systems and the whole area glowed like mounds of radiant, sparkling diamonds. Joy beyond human comprehension engulfed me and my aura blazed like a super nova bursting with delight.

"This whole cluster of stars and the millions of planets that encircle them is the Disney World of the Milky Way galaxy. If you could imagine heaven from the perspective of the human mind and multiply that by a thousand, you would be near the reality of the existence that those who live here are experiencing. This is where all souls from planets like Earth want to be. However, this is not the pinnacle of existence, not even near it. This is a physical and spiritual paradise and there are many dimensions of physical and spiritual realities above this one. This place is also a staging area where some of the people who leave Earth and Earth-type planets come for a short stay after they die. From here, most will be sent to other planets in the galaxy or back to Earth. A lucky few will remain here indefinitely, or until they move higher up to other realms of existence."

"Why do I get to see all this, Milton? Why am I privy to the things you are sharing with me today?"

"There are forces that don't want this information in the open, meaning on Earth. Others feel some of the people on Earth are ready for this kind of knowledge—not everything, just a few basics. Like the fact that life exists in many places in the solar system and throughout the galaxy. The entities I represent want faster technological growth and to lift the curtain of mystery up a notch or two, so that more humans can become aware and mature faster. Other entities do not want any revelations out at all and prefer a more austere, Dark Age existence for all people on Earth. We are in a vicious tug of war over agendas. We have sustained setbacks on our side about these differences. I have taken you out here to shield your physical being and for other unexplainable reasons that you would not understand even if I told you. You are a vessel, a container, as are thousands of others on Earth, where we keep certain DNA information and pertinent mental-imaged knowledge stored in various parts of your anatomy. We retrieve that material for use on Earth and other places in the cosmos that are under our watch. Everything we do pertains to human soul development."

"If I understand this correctly, I and others like me are part of a shell game between your forces and the other competing forces. You hide information within us and shuffle us around so that we remain concealed from them. Tell me, Milton, do you and those in your group try to infiltrate the other side with the same zeal?"

"We have made you difficult to tract down, but we have covered our bets by hiding similar information in others like you. Nevertheless, each member has unique information, which can only be deciphered with the correct combination of individuals such as yourself. You are a code, so we keep you people scattered all over the solar system. We increased our efforts to shield you and the others these last few years, even going as far as exposing you as a bluff to throw them off your tracks. We don't operate as they do. They are attempting to keep information and technology out of Earth, or to slow it down significantly by political shenanigans. So they have nothing to hide other than their motives."

"Is this a galactic Cold War? And if I were captured what would they do with me?"

"Cold War is a fair analogy. Unfortunately, our Cold Wars never end. If they capture you, they will most likely attempt to put you in storage for a time. The other side might try to manipulate the information hidden inside you and then possibly turn you loose with corrupted information. They could kill your body. But then things could get complicated for them because they would have to figure out who replaced you. That would not be easy. The other side might prefer to keep you trapped in your body instead. You are easier to track that way."

"Was it them that tried to kill me when I was in the bowels of the tube city? Moreover, what is keeping them from capturing my soul as you have done with me? For instance, you have taken me out of my body and now I'm helplessly tethered to you."

"Those who attempted to kill you were lower level humans who believed you were spying on them and have no connection with the entities I'm discussing. These extraterrestrial entities cannot capture your soul; they lack the authority and the capability to do so. Every entity or human soul is in a category. You, Michael, are at a level that they cannot hold on to, but they can capture your physical form and hold you for a certain amount of time while they attempt to erase information from you, or corrupt it."

Technology is nothing more than a higher level of understanding and it is not the evil that many like to make it out to be.

10

STAR CLUSTER

In a blink, Milton takes me to a planet with multiple suns revolving around each other like electrons around an atom. The planet we traveled to was located on the periphery of its sun, as Uranus is on our solar system. There were twenty planets and hundreds of moons in that solar system. A flurry of interplanetary travel was taking place with many types of colorful ships coming and going at dazzling speeds and maneuvers. The ships were traveling to and from various moons, space cities and other planets in that multiple solar system. As we came nearer to the flurry of ships and other strange-looking objects that were of various sizes and shapes, they took on the appearance of confetti swirling and twirling in rapid succession creating symbols and images that provoked wondrous feelings of delight in my soul.

"Milton, is there something special going on down on the planet? Or is what I am seeing and feeling the normal everyday activity for this place?"

"This is typical festivities that never subside, but ebb and flow indefinitely like ocean waves on a beach. Are you ready to join in the fun, Michael?"

I never answered because I was not sure what that entailed. Would a bunch of freaky type aliens that looked like Milton surround me and then laugh at Milton's little catch? That was on my mind and I knew Milton could read my mind and he did not respond to my thoughts as he often did, which worried me.

We dropped like lead balloons from hundreds of miles above the planet and entered into a cube-type structure in what presumably was a city. Inside the cube were several swarms of glowing entities as far as my eyes could see, but I did not have eyes. I was a glowing ball like the rest of them and I could see there were big swarms and little swarms of various degrees of luminosity, like small versions of the star clusters. These clusters of souls brimmed with life and shear momentum as swarms of bees around hives drenched in honey. Milton headed for one of the swarms with me in tow. It was an orgy of pure love, happiness and banter. I instantly remembered every entity in the swarm and there were countless hundreds of them. They were friends and family from other lifetimes and places during my entire existence in the galaxy.

Communication with them was phenomenally simple. I was in contact with each individual in the swarm all at the same time with no confusion of thought. I had multi-faceted communications capabilities—certainly not possible while inside a human brain. I was as fully aware of hundreds of entities as they were also fully aware of me. It was non-stop pleasure, no disagreements, no misunderstanding, only pure social engagement at its finest and truest form. Some of the entities were there briefly, having taken a short break from their lives on other worlds as I had. Others have been there for hundreds and thousands of Earth years, never tiring of the social intercourse. I felt as if I had never left, as if I awoke from a dream or deep sleep.

The swarm was an ongoing family gathering without end or a climax. Individuals came and departed as if they were electrons jumping in and out of the surface of an atom, while the nucleus of souls remained intact. Millions of such family swarms existed inside countless cube structures that covered the surface of that planet, a planet twice the size of Jupiter. Outside of the cubes were many physical types of beings, as well as many levels of ethereal entities. Every conceivable way of life was represented on the multiple planets and moons in that solar system, as well as on the millions of other solar systems in that star cluster.

I realized then that Milton was family and one with a very close attachment to me. I also noticed that my tether to Milton during my stay on that planet was gone and I was free to go wherever I pleased. While in the swarm, I felt an inexplicable pull from another member who was not in attendance and I chose to fade out of the party and pursue my impulse to find that person. I instantly went to one of my favorite places on that planet. It was a luxurious house with marble columns and fabulous paintings and tapestries decorating the walls. The house was reminiscent of Romanesque palaces of European aristocracies.

I was a radiant orb. Yet, while in that house, I felt as if I were inside my physical body again, the one I left on the moon orbiting Uranus. I felt, and could see, my hands and I walked out of the house and into the courtyard as if I had my legs back. The courtyard was covered with manicured gardens filled with fragrant flowers and sumptuous ripe fruit that dangled from vines. Birds chirped and sang in the trees and butterflies danced in the midst of a perfect, sunlit day. It was a wonderful place, a garden in paradise.

As I strolled through the grounds admiring the many varieties of plants, I spotted a woman tending the garden and walked over to her. She looked up at me with a large smile on her face and not at all surprised by my being there, it was as if she had been expecting me. She stood up, grabbed my face with her warm smooth petite hands, and kissed it all over. Then she spoke to me.

"Michael, my adorable grandchild! I heard you were here! I summoned you to visit with me and here you are! How wonderful you look!"

"Grandmother! It has been ages since I saw you last. Yet, it seems only yesterday that I was playing in your garden as a child in our Italian village. You look the same as you did back then, vibrant and beautiful."

"It's a pity you must leave so soon, Michael, but your time away from here is short and you will be back here for a long period. I'm looking forward to your quick return, Michael. There are so many things we must talk about."

My grandmother saw me in a physical form as if I were in my human body.

"Where is grandfather? Does he live with you?"

"He is living on another planet somewhere in the galaxy and will not be released for another forty Earth years. I do not know at this time if he will come here or go to another life. I visit him sometimes in his dreams to give him encouragement."

"But you are in a physical body. Can you also travel in the spirit to visit people in their dreams?"

"I can with the assistance of family members like Milton, the same way you are here with me now. You do know that you are in my dream don't you?"

I was stunned at hearing that revelation.

"I'm only a dream to you?"

"Dreams here are not like dreams on Earth, Michael. When we dream, we are awake. We never sleep here. Nevertheless, I am in a physical state and you are a spirit. I can see and touch your spirit as if you were in a physical body. It's impossible to explain these things to you. Your soul/mind remains blocked from many things until you return to this place permanently."

"Do you miss grandpa while he is away?"

"Sorrow has no place in this plane of existence because no one really departs. It is no different from someone on Earth going off to work and then returning home that evening. Time has no relevance for us, either. We exist in a blissful, consistent state of clarity. We enjoy the company of family members as I am now doing with you and I indulge in the things that I love, like tending my flower gardens. I also take pleasure in beautiful artwork and architecture. And as you can see, I surround myself with the things I love. Everyone in this place does what they love most."

She kissed me and gave me a big hug and instantly I was transported back to Milton inside of the swarm.

(Speaking to Milton) "I'm sad that I didn't get more time to spend with grandmother. Why wasn't I allowed more time with her?"

"The visit you just had is not normally permitted, but the moment she realized you were near, she insisted on seeing you and she brought you to her."

"Why isn't she here in the swarm with the other family members?"

"The family is much larger than what is in the swarm. You have family in many places and on many levels, both physical and spiritual domains. Your grandmother remained in a physical region by choice, on a planet in this system that is nearer to one of the suns."

Milton retreated from the swarm and tugged me along with him, so my freedom was short. We paused above the planet with the cubes on it for a last look. In that moment of departure, I instantly felt the pain that inflicts most humans when we leave loved ones behind.

"Milton, do you feel the immense sadness I am feeling right now?"

"I feel the pain for you, but I am with them much of the time and I am not departing from them as you are. You are returning to a world where most live out their lives in darkness. In my world, I am never far from the light of family love. I do my job and at the end of the day— allegorically speaking, I know everything is good, regardless of the outcome on places such as Earth. In your present state of existence, much remains hidden from you, Michael, but that is all by design. However, you now know parts of the big picture and you will retain these memories when I return you to Earth, a rare privilege."

INSIDE DOME

I saw my body sleeping soundly on the bed. A sight difficult to get my mind around, it was as if I was in two places at once and surprisingly, I was ok with that. I loved the idea of being free from my body. The mere though of having to reenter my body was repulsive and terrifying.

"Do I have to go back into that 'thing,' Milton?"

"Afraid so. You have stuff to do back on Earth that will not get done until you do it."

Milton entered into his body with ease, grabbed my orb, and shoved it into my physical head without giving me additional time to think about it. My body jumped back to life and I once again found myself entombed inside of it.

"I feel like a ton of bricks! This body sucks, Milton. Can I lay here and recuperate for a little while?"

"That's the problem of being outside of your body for any length of time. The longer you're out, the more difficult it is to readjust to it."

"This is like the worst hangover ever. Is there something I can take for it?"

"Believe it or not, the discomfort you are experiencing is the best and quickest remedy. There is no other way to readjust to the body. In addition, your body needs to heal from your absence on the psychological and the physiological realm."

"I feel like I've been working in the salt mines for a week with open sores, but why? My heart continued to pump blood to my body and my body looked like it was sleeping peacefully before I reentered it, like a car left idling, so why do I feel like a truck ran over me?"

"Your body was peaceful, Michael, but that's only good for the dead. Your body needs to move around while you sleep. Movement keeps the blood from stagnating and getting cutoff from certain areas. Without your spirit inside the body to keep it restless, the body is technically dead. No dreams or movements take place. You have not been out of your body more than twenty minutes; therefore, no lasting damage occurred. Had you been away much longer, a mechanical masseuse would have gone to work on your body, massaging it to stimulate blood circulation. We also, in certain situations, insert a 'temp' entity to keep the body warm."

"If there was an android or mechanical masseuse in this place, why didn't it pick up my body and place it onto the bed? Why did you have to do it? And thank you for not giving me any more details about the temp. That sounds way too creepy."

"Concerning the android and why I didn't have it do the work for us, I wanted to demonstrate to you that spirits have the ability to move solid objects. Although you were an orb of pure energy, you had the means to lift your body and affect other physical objects as well. We can do this by physical contact as well as telekinetically. However, I will leave that for another day. Also, that temp thing is not as bad as it sounds, but I will not go into details during today's session."

"How about shipping my body back to Earth and let me fly there and reunite with it there?"

"I could allow that if you weren't carrying certain objects inside of you. Don't ask about the objects because I will not tell you. Nevertheless, you have been off the nest long enough and must return to your body to keep things from spoiling."

"Sit on the nest! That sounds so not right, Milton! Couldn't you have phrased that another way?"

"The few minutes you were out of your body were not critical, but the objects need to be wired to your spirit mind to remain viable, is that better?"

"Yeah, that is more palatable, but what is it that I'm carrying inside of me Milton?"

"It's something that will chew its way out of your chest once we enter Earth's atmosphere and spread rapidly like a super virus infecting the whole planet Earth. I told you not to ask me."

"I assume you are joking with me, but how do I know you are kidding? You may have implanted all those cushy memories about family into my head. How can I be sure of anything after seeing what you are capable of doing? You are at the very least a wizard, but you also have the power and knowledge of a god."

"We must keep an element of doubt alive in you for this operation to remain workable. Getting you back to Earth is not a slam-dunk. If the other side captures you, it is best that you have fragmented knowledge of the operation and plenty of ambiguity for them to dig through. They do not extract information by interrogation. They scan every cell in your brain and body looking for patterns. From these biological and psychological fingerprints, they can determine where you have been, the planets and places in this solar system or even if you left the solar system. These entities can determine many things from the food you have consumed, the air you breathe, and the gravitational pull on your body are all clues to your journey. My job is to try and remain one step ahead of them."

"If I'm captured can't they simply remove the items inside of me during my abduction and then wipe my memory clean of it?"

"You are past that stage. They cannot simply drop in, abduct you, and then turn you loose as if nothing ever happened. The items inside of you are hard-wired into you and only we can extract them. Their main concern is stopping what you have from entering Earth. They probably will not kill you, but they will damage the items if they can, and maybe take you. Depends on who gets to you first, a human covert organization or other extraterrestrials. Your body is designed to transport these things. Humans may not notice that fact, but higher up entities can. Therefore, the items are not the only things at risk. You are too."

"If that is the case, why don't I get around-the-clock protection from your people, Milton?"

"We have to keep our distance. Otherwise, we will give your location away. We are easier to detect than you are and where there is smoke there is fire—you. However, your classification will change after you get back to Earth and you will no longer be a courier for us and a target for them."

"When are we going back to Earth? Are you waiting for a window of sorts?"

"Yes, the timing for reentry is important. Getting back on earth is not as simple as getting out of Earth. We are taking a direct flight into Earth, like a laser beam. As soon as everything lines up, we go."

"So I'm not returning to Earth the way I got here? And what has to 'line up'?"

"You are traveling in my ship this time. There is protocol for getting into Earth, like passports and customs. But don't worry. I will take care of all those minor details for you."

"So, what you are saying is that you have to smuggle me back in? And your little ship has the power to travel long distance at more than the speed of light?"

"That little ship of mine manipulates gravity and magnetic waves which cause it to become very slippery inside the fabric of space. I will explain it to you in more detail someday. Yes, I have to smuggle you back into Earth. Now let's enter my ship."

Milton levitated into the opening of his ship that was docked to the dome, and then pointed at me from inside the ship and levitated me into the ship.

"Wow, where can I get a finger like that, Milton?"

"Perhaps on your next assignment, Michael."

RETURN TO EARTH

Once inside the craft, the opening closed and Milton and I walked towards the center of the ship. An opening appeared and we entered into a foggy area. Milton then led me to a section that had compartments that looked similar to those in the large transport, in which I traveled to Uranus. Except these were vertical compartments with standing room only. Milton pointed to one of the compartments and asked me to enter it.

I entered the vertical cubicle and then I turned to look out at Milton and it closed around me. Instantly the compartment filled with a foamy substance and I lost consciousness. I then immediately regained consciousness and my spirit was outside of the cubicle, but my essence or spirit could not move from that spot. I didn't know if I remained attached to my body or if I was inserted into some device that was next to my body. I was aware of the haze that engulfed the room and I could see my body encased in a foam type of substance, but I was not inside my body.

The ship pulled away from the glass dome and vanished into the darkness of space. Moments later, it pierced Earth's atmosphere and the craft hovered next to my car in the parking lot where I had left it that morning. It was dark outside, except for the dim light from two street lamps. There were three cars a hundred yards from where my car was. Teenagers were making out inside the cars. Some were sitting on the hoods. Others were sprawled on the grass drinking beer, smoking cigarettes, and talking. None of them seemed to notice the ship hovering next to my car. Apparently, Milton blocked the ship from their view or we were cloaked. I jumped down out of Milton's ship that hovered about two feet from the ground and got into my car. I realized then that my space-watch was gone and my old watch was back on my wrist and displayed the time that I had entered the ship that morning. I shook my head in disbelief, started my car, and noticed the clock on the dashboard displayed the time 11:45 PM. Milton's ship darted away into another dimension. I pulled out of the parking lot and drove home.

Debbie, my wife, was sitting in the living room reading a book when I walked through the door.

"Hi, honey. Sorry I'm late getting home. I was abducted by aliens this morning while walking in the park, and they just let me go!"

"Oh, so that's where you were. Your office called and made up some cockamamie story that you were with clients. I didn't believe them."

(I laughed) "Anyway, I'm tired, are you ready for bed?"

"Yes, let's go."

She put down her book, turned off the reading lamp and we headed up the stairs to the bedroom. At the top of the landing, I grabbed her and gave her a long passionate kiss.

Debbie, surprised by my display of affection, melted into my arms.

"I guess you are not all that tired, Mike?"

I did not answer her, but had a devilish grin on my face. I lifted her up into my arms and carried her into the bedroom, as I once did many years ago when I was a younger and stronger man. I put her down next to the bed and removed her clothing. She unbuttoned my shirt. We tumbled onto the bed and fell in love all over again. The love was magical and continued for more than an hour before we both fell asleep embraced as one.

THE NEXT MORNING

That morning I was up early as usual. I made a pot of coffee, sat down at the breakfast table, and read the newspaper. I was trying to read the paper, but my mind was absorbed in what I had experienced the day before. Debbie came into the kitchen in her robe, poured herself a cup of coffee, sat down at the table next to me and with a large smile on her face glanced over at me. In her sexy voice, she asked me, "What was that all about last night? Was that you or someone else?"

"Not sure, honey. As a matter of fact, I'm not sure about a lot of things this morning."

"What's that suppose to mean? Last night was beyond wonderful. Now you're talking as if you are going through a midlife crisis?"

She reached over, took my hands and clasped hers over mine as a gesture of affection.

"I want you to tell me that it was you, that the fire remains alive in our relationship. Did something happen at the office yesterday that you are withholding from me? Did you lose an important account? You can tell me anything, you know."

"Nothing happened at the office and the fire is far from going out, baby! However, last night was a bit of a surprise for me as well."

"Then what is it that is bothering you?"

"You know I have mentioned being abducted in the past by extraterrestrials? Well, it happened again yesterday."

Sarcastically she responded: "I know you are an alien, dear. I have known it since I married you, but can't you come up with anything better?"

She got up from the table, went to the refrigerator and pulled out a carton of eggs and a package of bacon.

"Feel like breakfast, dear?"

"Yes, please, haven't had breakfast at home in sometime; sounds great, do we have bread for toast?"

Without waiting for an answer, I got up from the table and rummaged through the cabinets as if I were unfamiliar with where things were in the kitchen.

"Don't bother looking, we are out of bread, we hardly ever use it so I stopped buying it. I assume you are not going to the office this morning since you're still here?"

"I'm taking the day off, or maybe the whole week, I need to hash out something in my head."

"Good, maybe we can go out and do something together this afternoon but I have a strange pain in my abdomen that was bothering me all night, so I'm going to call my gynecologist and see if she can get me in this morning for a quick checkup."

"Why didn't you tell me about the pain last night? We did get a little out there, perhaps you pulled a muscle?"

"That's why I didn't say anything, but the pain has increased so it wouldn't hurt to see what my doctor has to say."

"Well, ok, let me know what she tells you and perhaps later on in the day we can do something together, whatever you want to do baby!"

I finished my breakfast and I got up from the table, kissed Debbie and went downstairs to my study.

I telepathically called out to Milton: "Milton, can you hear me?"

No answer.

I wanted to dismiss my experiences as a dream or hallucination, but I could not. I was not asleep, nor do I use drugs, so it was not something I imagined. I went to the park yesterday morning after eating breakfast at one the local eateries as I had done many times. Moreover, I was now in possession of information that could change the underpinnings of everything humans believe to be true in this life! Like the big three cornerstones of humanity: religion, history and the sciences. What to do with that information was now on my mind, but who would believe any of it?

Debbie shouted from the hallway down to me, "Honey, I talked to my gynecologist and she said to come in this morning. She seemed concerned with what I told her, so I'm going now, talk to you when I get back, love you."

I ran up the stairs to catch her before she left.

"Do you want me to go with you dear?"

"No, I will be fine."

She blew a kiss at me. I was standing in the stairway and blew a kiss back to her. I then return to my den to continue pondering my new reality.

TWO HOURS LATER

I am sitting in my den working on my computer when I hear the front door open. Debbie was back from her appointment. She walked down the steps to my den and stood in the doorway. I looked up from my computer screen and asked, "Did they find anything?"

"The gynecologist found some strange lumps in my uterus, but as she examined the lumps they detached and she was able to extract them with an instrument. The moment she removed them the pain went away. She showed them to me, they were dime size cysts. Everything else checked out fine."

I got up from my chair, went over to her, and gave her a hug.

"That is great honey! Now we have the rest of the day to do whatever you want to do."

GYNECOLOGICAL OFFICE

(Gynecologist speaking telepathically to Milton) "Milton, I have extracted the embryos from Debbie. I can insert one at 2 PM and the other at 3 PM, does it matter which woman gets which, or are they identical embryos this time?"

Milton responds, "They are identical. The embryos that are replaced will be picked up when you tell me they are ready."

"They will be ready shortly after the second appointment."